PENCILVANIA

PENCILVANIA

STEPHANIE WATSON

Illustrated by SOFIA MOORE

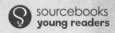

sourcebooks
young readers

Published by Sourcebooks Young Readers, an imprint of Sourcebooks Kids
P.O. Box 4410, Naperville, Illinois 60567-4410
(630) 961-3900
sourcebookskids.com

Library of Congress Cataloging-in-Publication data is on file with the publisher.

Source of Production: Sheridan Books, Chelsea, Michigan, United States of America
Date of Production: August 2021
Run Number: 5022539

Printed and bound in the United States of America.
SB 10 9 8 7 6 5 4 3 2 1

For Lisa

1

Ever since she first learned to hold a crayon, Zora loved
to draw.

She drew circles and lines, filling page after page. As she
grew, she learned to draw suns and rainbows and people and
trees and skyscrapers. She used markers and colored pencils
and pens and oil pastels to fill sketchbook after sketchbook.
For Zora, everything was worth drawing, and drawing was
everything.

Twelve-year-old Zora sprawled on the sunny dining room floor, her sketchbook open to a blank page. She dug in the tub of art supplies beside her and chose an orange pencil. A single spark ignited in her chest, just like it always  did when she drew. The spark burst into countless balls of light that sped around inside her, a million possible drawings bumping into each other. Zora touched the pencil to the paper, and the first line zipped across it like a firework climbing to the very top of the sky. Then pictures exploded onto the paper, one after another.

The living room disappeared. The sound of Zora's mom and little sister, Frankie, dancing to Prince's "Purple Rain" faded. Time stopped. The world became only the fast-moving pencil, the paper, and the pictures pouring out.

Lying on the sun-drenched floor, Zora drew her family's little blue house, which sat high on the hill in Duluth, Minnesota, overlooking Lake

Superior. She'd lived there her whole life and had drawn the house dozens of times. She drew a storm of purple raindrops. She drew a robot with a light bulb for a head.

"Zora." Mom rubbed quick circles on Zora's back, breaking her trance. "Aren't you hungry? You've been drawing all afternoon."

"I'm almost...done." Zora added the final stroke to her drawing of a deer with forks for antlers. She put down the pencil, and the world came rushing back. Zora's little sister was sitting on the couch reading *Horse Sense*, her giant book of horse facts.

Zora gazed out the wide front window at Lake Superior. In the land of ten thousand lakes, this lake was by far the biggest. It was so huge, you couldn't see across it. The setting sun painted the steel-gray water with hot pink and periwinkle and turned the clouds to copper and gold.

Mom bent down to look at the deer in Zora's sketchbook, her long, dark curls touching the paper.

"I love that its antlers are forks," Mom said. "Your Voom is on fire today."

Voom. That's what Mom and Zora called the warm, tingly spark inside that said *draw draw draw*. Zora had felt it for as long as she could remember. Mom had Voom too. Once, Zora asked her if it was magic. Yes and no, Mom had said. Everyone has Voom, but some people use it to dance or skateboard or build Lego villages instead of draw. It's both special and ordinary.

"Draw me a horse!" Frankie said, galloping over from the couch. She clutched the book of horse facts to her chest. She got it last month for her sixth birthday, and she had already read it so many times that the cover was battered, the corners soft.

"*Another* horse?" Zora laughed and flipped to a fresh page in her sketchbook. "What color?"

"Blue."

"What kind of blue?" Zora asked. There were so many. "Sky blue, teal, cornflower, cobalt, navy..." She loved how each color variation had its own special name.

"You pick," Frankie said.

Zora chose a cobalt-blue marker from the tub and started sketching. Frankie sat cross-legged next to her and opened *Horse Sense*.

"Did you know," Frankie read, "the fastest horse speed ever recorded was fifty-five miles per hour?"

"Get outta town," Mom said. "That's as fast as a car. Zora, can you believe that?"

"I don't just believe it. I'm *drawing* it." She drew muscular blue legs running full throttle, the blue tail flying out like a flag.

"Did you know," Frankie read, "some horses can grow a mustache?"

"For real?" Mom sank to the floor next to Zora, like she was too shocked to stand anymore. "That's *adorable*." She sounded breathless with amazement. Zora laughed. Mom was always good at playing along.

Zora added a bright-blue mustache to the end of the horse's nose. She drew a realistic eye, which seemed to watch her as she shaded the body, adding lines where the muscles bulged from running so fast. Zora could practically feel the horse's heart beating hard in its chest.

"She's beautiful," Frankie breathed, peering at the drawing. "I wish I could ride her."

Mom pointed at Frankie and shut one eye. "Next year, baby."

Frankie's number one dream was to ride a horse. Mom promised she could when she turned seven. Eat your veggies and get a little taller and older, Mom said. Then you can take riding lessons.

Frankie crawled onto the couch to study more horse facts and shout out the best ones. (Horses have 205 bones! The average horse heart weighs ten pounds!) Mom grabbed her own sketchbook off the dining room table. *Twist, twist, twist* went Mom's pencil sharpener. Zora inhaled the sweet, woody scent of the pencil coming to a point. It was Mom's signature smell.

Zora watched as Mom whisked the pencil lightly over the paper, leaving only a few wispy lines. The image of Frankie sitting on the couch emerged from the white fog of the paper. She even captured the quirk of Frankie's pursed lips as she read.

Zora leaned back on her hands, admiring the sketch. "How do you do that?"

"Do what?"

"Make her look so real." It was like a magic trick.

Mom laughed and turned to a new page in her sketch-book. She scooted to face Zora. "You want to know the secret?"

Zora nodded and sat up straighter.

Mom locked eyes with Zora and started to sweep her pencil across the paper.

"When I draw," she said—*sweep, sweep*—"I really look at my subject and draw the truth of what I see. If you do that, even if your drawing isn't *technically* perfect, it will be perfectly truthful. Because you will have captured the essence of what you're drawing."

Mom turned her sketchbook to face Zora, and Zora met the gaze of the girl on the paper. It wasn't the same exact face Zora saw when she looked in the mirror or at a photo of herself. But it was her. It looked how she felt on the inside.

"It's me," Zora whispered.

Mom carefully tore the page from the spiral binding and handed it to Zora.

"Just draw the truth, huh?" Zora said.

"Yep. Which, by the way, you already know how to do."

Mom pointed up at the picture frames crowding the dining room wall. The Permanent Collection, Mom called it. "You've always drawn the truth of what you see in your imagination. Your drawings are powerful."

Zora scanned the frames on the wall. Her eyes landed on a hamster slumber party scene, with hundreds of hamsters in pajamas. Zora went through an epic hamster-drawing phase when she was eight. *Hammies in Jammies*, Mom called that picture.

"It's the same when you draw from real life," Mom said. "Just draw what you see." She closed her sketchbook with a joyful slap. "Well, ladies, I'm starving. And because I'm the queen of this castle, I have decided that we shall have breakfast for dinner." She held up a regal finger.

"YES!" Zora cheered.

"Woo-hoo!" Frankie leapt off the couch. Breakfast for dinner meant going to the all-you-can-eat pancake house down by the lift bridge, right on the water's edge. A cozy booth and steaming stacks of fluffy pancakes and three kinds of syrup.

Zora tucked her sketchbook under her arm and grabbed

her jacket from the hall closet. Frankie sat on the floor to put on her shoes.

"Hey," Mom said, rattling the car keys in her coat pocket. "I have to tell you two something at dinner."

Frankie looked up. "At *breakfast*, you mean."

Mom grinned. "Right."

At the restaurant, they placed their usual order—buttermilk pancakes and orange juice. Then Mom folded her hands under her chin and looked across the table at Zora and Frankie.

"So. Remember when I went to the doctor last week?" Mom asked.

Frankie nodded. "We waited in the lobby, and I got a green lollipop."

"Right. Well, they did some blood tests," Mom said. "And today, the doctor called with the results. It turns out I have leukemia."

"Leukemia?" Zora spit out the word like it tasted bad. "Isn't that, like, blood cancer?"

"Yes, but Zora, don't freak out." Mom reached across the table and squeezed Zora's hand.

The ravenous hunger Zora had felt a moment ago turned into a pit in her stomach. Leukemia was one of the worst kinds of cancers, wasn't it?

"Don't freak out about what?" Frankie asked, putting down the syrup bottle she was playing with.

"Look: I have leukemia, but I am going to kick its butt. Hard." Mom shook her head slowly. "It's gonna be sooo sorry it came for me."

Frankie giggled, and so did Mom. Not Zora.

"Are you getting treatment?" Zora asked.

"Of course. Chemotherapy starts next week," Mom said and rattled Zora's hand. "*Don't worry*. I'm going to be fine. I promise."

Zora took a deep breath, filling her lungs with the sweet vanilla-flavored air of the pancake house. Mom always made good on her promises, whether it was to take them out for pizza after school or pick up a new sketchbook for Zora. They could count on Mom this time too. But...leukemia? The more Zora repeated the strange word in her head, the more it sounded like the name of a comic book supervillain.

The waiter appeared then, carrying a tray loaded with three steaming plates of pancakes.

"Food's here!" Mom said, sounding too cheerful. She reached for the pitcher of syrup and drenched her pancakes. Frankie dove into her plate. But Zora wasn't hungry. She moved her plate to one side and opened her sketchbook on the sticky table. The Voom ignited and swelled inside her, and the pencil started moving.

Zora drew Mom's face wearing a don't-mess-with-me expression. She sketched an orange cape draped around incredibly muscular shoulders. Thick, powerful thighs in orange tights and blue rubber boots. Zora imagined the superheroic Mom punching the villainous Leukemia in the face.

Pow!

"Who's that?" Mom asked, pointing her fork at Zora's drawing.

"You?" Zora said hopefully.

Mom winked at her. "Dang right it is."

2

Nine months had passed since that pancake dinner.

Zora sat on the edge of Mom's hospital bed, picking fluff off the cotton blanket covering Mom's bony legs. Her room at Allegheny General Hospital in Pittsburgh, Pennsylvania, was all grays and blacks and whites, as if it were sketched in pencil. The room smelled like a giant Band-Aid.

Frankie sat on a gray vinyl chair eating a cup of cottage cheese from Mom's lunch tray. Lately, Mom never finished her tray.

"I miss Lake Superior," Frankie said. "When are we going home?" Duluth was almost a thousand miles away.

When Mom's doctor said she needed yet another round of chemo and would have to stay in the hospital for a while this time, Mom flew them to Pittsburgh, where Grandma Wren lived. They'd only been in Pennsylvania for two weeks, but it seemed way longer.

"We're going home soon, baby," Mom said and smiled at Frankie. Her face was so thin, the dimples in her cheeks had vanished. Instead of smelling like sweet pencil shavings, she reeked of antiseptic soap and chemicals.

"When we get back, let's go camping," Frankie said.

"You're reading my mind, Frankie," Mom said. "Camping up north sounds amazing."

They had to miss the last few days of school to come to Pennsylvania. It was summer vacation now, but it sure didn't feel like it.

A rumbly clatter echoed down the hallway.

"Meal cart!" Frankie cried. "I'm gonna see if they have extra cookies."

Frankie dashed into the hall after the noisy cart. Zora stayed in the room and listened to another sound: the *boop-boop* of Mom's heart monitor. She watched the IV bag drip mysterious fluid into Mom's veins. Zora felt fire in hers.

If the chemo treatments were working like Mom said they were, why was she becoming more frail and breathless every day? And if all those magical remedies like sleeping with crystals under her pillow and listening to Tibetan bowl music and chanting affirmations like *I am the perfect picture of health* were actually helping, then why was Mom turning into a drawing of a stick figure?

She was bald under her blue flowered scarf. The last of her long, brown curls had dropped out weeks ago. An air tube snaked out of her nose and across her neck.

"I don't want to live with Grandma Wren," Zora said. "Her apartment smells weird. She plays bad music."

Mom laughed, but almost no sound came out. "Come on, you don't like jazz?"

Zora crossed her arms. "No." And another thing: "How come she never came to visit us in Duluth?"

"She hates flying. But she did come a few years back. Remember? We went to Canal Park and watched ore boats."

"Not really," Zora said. What was she then, six years old? That was half her life ago.

"I remember we were sitting on our back porch, and she told you that Wren was the name of a bird," Mom said. "You drew her this funny-looking green bird wearing her big glasses. She couldn't stop laughing."

Zora didn't remember any bird wearing glasses. Aside from that short visit, a card on her birthday, and the occasional hello on the phone, Grandma Wren was a stranger.

"My mom is really cool once you get to know her," Mom

said. "Too bad you won't get the chance. We're going back to Duluth in a week or two."

"How do you know?" Zora was too scared to ask the real question: *What if you die?*

"Come here, baby." Mom pulled Zora into a tight, bony hug.

Tears sprang to Zora's eyes. Her heart raced. Finally, *finally* they were going to talk about it—the terrible possibility that Mom might not recover.

Mom squeezed Zora and whispered in her ear. "Listen: the leukemia is strong, but *I am stronger*. Remember that superhero picture you drew of me? I'm gonna beat this."

Darkness roiled and swirled inside Zora, like a whirlpool dragging her down deep inside of herself. After all of Mom's big talk about drawing the truth, why was she avoiding the truth now? Zora saw the highway of tubes traveling in and out of Mom's body. She saw the nurses' *poor thing* looks over their shoulders as they left the room.

Mom wouldn't talk about dying. But it could happen. And if it did, what would they do without her?

"Draw me a picture," Mom said.

Zora leveled her eyes at Mom. "I don't know what to draw." The Voom had grown faint the last few weeks, like a song playing in a room down the hall. The only thing she felt like drawing lately was Lake Superior—page after page filled with blue. But right now, she didn't even want to draw the lake.

"You could sketch me." Mom sat up straighter against her pillow and centered the collar of her gray hospital gown. "Draw me standing by the lake. I'm in a beautiful red dress. I have long hair that's blowing in the breeze." She ran a skeletal hand over her headscarf, which fell onto her pillow.

Zora slapped open her sketchbook to a clean page. Today, she wouldn't draw Mom like she used to look—strong and healthy. She wouldn't draw a superhero either. Zora would draw the truth of what Mom was now: Skinny. Pale. Bald. Let her see how seriously sick she was. Maybe then she'd stop pretending and say the words that Zora both dreaded and needed to hear: *If I die...*

Zora dragged her pencil tip in a circle on the paper. She

drew the perfect truth of Mom's head: too big for her body, no hair. She added a spindly neck.

Her gaze flitted between the paper and Mom's face, so she could get the details just right. She drew arms made into sharp angles by the leukemia. Eyes with half-moon shadows lurking underneath.

Frankie ran into the room, shaking a package of cookies triumphantly over her head. "Score!"

Zora blinked back tears as she sketched Mom's scrawny knees huddled under the hospital blanket.

"Is my picture ready?" Mom asked.

Frankie leaned in for a look at the drawing. "Ew. You're not going to like it."

"If Zora made it, I will."

"No, Frankie's right," Zora said, her voice as flat as paper. She turned the sketchbook to face Mom. *See how sick you are, then tell us the truth*, Zora wanted to shout. Instead, she pressed her lips into a straight line.

Mom studied the picture for a long moment. Then she gave Zora a small, sad smile.

Zora met her eyes but refused to smile back. She got up,

walked out of the room, and waited in the lobby till Grandma Wren came for them.

That night, Zora lay in her top bunk at Grandma Wren's, a hollow feeling spreading in her stomach. She imagined Mom all alone in her hospital bed. *Yeah, I was mad, but would it have been so hard to smile back?* What if Mom thought Zora hated her? *Tomorrow, I'll say sorry.*

The door to the bedroom opened a crack, letting in a blade of light from the hall. "Zora?" Grandma Wren whispered. "Are you still awake?"

"Yeah. What is it?"

Grandma Wren took a deep breath. "Your mom..."

Before Grandma Wren said anything else, Zora knew.

Mom was gone.

The Voom vanished that same night, even though Mom always said it was impossible to lose it. Another lie.

Now, Zora could never say sorry. And she could never change the fact that Mom had smiled at her and she hadn't smiled back.

3

Scuff, scuff. Zora turned from where she sat on the top bunk toward the tiny window near the ceiling. Inches from Zora's face, a pair of rubber rain boots shuffled by. Grandma Wren's basement apartment in Pittsburgh was "garden level," which sounded fancy. But what it really meant was that the apartment was buried underground, like a body in a graveyard.

Two months. That's how long it had been since Mom died. Zora hadn't been able to draw anything since. The Voom was gone. If she even picked up a pencil to draw, her heart hammered. Her knees turned to water. Her vision blurred. And she felt like throwing up.

"Girls, I'll be ready in ten minutes!" Grandma Wren called in a gravelly voice from the kitchen. She had told them to go wait in their bedroom so she could prepare Frankie's birthday surprise.

Today was Frankie's seventh birthday.

"*Riding lessons!*" Frankie mouthed to Zora. She galloped around the braided rug.

Zora bit her lip. A couple weeks ago, Zora had told Grandma Wren in private about Mom's promise of riding lessons for Frankie's birthday. It would mean the world to Frankie, Zora said. Grandma Wren had sucked her teeth and said, "I don't know. I'll think about it." Everyone over the age of seven knows that means *no chance*.

Zora should've warned Frankie then to not get her hopes up, but she couldn't. Because Frankie's eyebrows would do that thing where they slanted down in disappointment, forming a pointy roof over her brown eyes. It made her face look like a sad little house.

Zora was powerless against Frankie's sad, pointy-roof eyebrows.

"Zora, will you make my mark?" Frankie held up Zora's tin of colored pencils.

Every birthday, Mom had marked their height on the kitchen doorjamb. Frankie was obsessed with growing older and taller. The sooner she got older, the sooner she could ride horses. And she wanted to be tall enough to get on a horse by herself.

Frankie shook the tin of pencils at Zora like a maraca, and the sound made Zora's heart race.

"Please?" Frankie said.

"You draw it," Zora said. "Seven-year-olds are big enough to make their own lines."

Frankie grinned and chose a red pencil from the tin. She pressed her back against the blank white doorframe, next to the stack of cardboard boxes from their move to Pittsburgh. The boxes were still taped shut. Zora tried not to look at them. Tried not to picture Mom's sketchbooks and sweaters folded inside. All of Zora's old drawings were in there too.

Frankie rested the pencil on top of her head and made a

bright red swipe on the doorframe. She stepped back to examine the line. "Did I get taller?"

Zora hopped down from the top bunk. "Definitely." But really, who knew? It's not like they could compare this line with the other ones. The marks from all their past birthdays were in their old house in Duluth. They were probably hidden under a fresh coat of paint by now.

Frankie covered her height line with her thumb. "I miss Mom," she said softly.

"Me too." Zora stretched one of Frankie's dark-brown curls and let it go. She missed everything about their old life. Their blue house in Duluth. Their friends. Lake Superior. Pittsburgh had zero lakes, unless you counted Panther Hollow, which was human-made and only slightly bigger than a puddle. A fake lake. It was August now, and Pittsburgh was as hot and humid as a mouth. Or a sweaty armpit. ArmPittsburgh. Zora's throat ached for Lake Superior, which was like a bottomless cold drink.

"If Mom were here, what would she say?" Frankie asked.

Zora slapped her hand to her chest with dramatic flair. "You grew *again*? Stop that!"

Frankie laughed.

Zora's smile faded. Pretending Mom was still alive and pretending to be happy, even for two seconds, made Zora's heart feel like it was in a trash compactor.

Frankie sat on her bottom bunk. She touched the piece of paper taped to the wall over her pillow; it was the fast blue horse with a mustache that Zora had sketched in Duluth. "Draw me a picture," Frankie said.

"I told you: I can't draw anymore. The Voom is gone."

"*Please?* Just one horse," Frankie begged. "It's my birthday."

Zora sighed. "Fine, I'll try." As she reached for her sketchbook, she prayed for even the tiniest bit of Voom. *Please. For Frankie.*

Zora opened the tin and chose a dark-purple pencil. Instead of a warm, tingly rush of Voom, a frantic feeling filled her chest. Her breaths grew tight and shallow, like her lungs were bound with rope. Her vision swam. Zora threw the pencil and sketchbook across the room. The panic faded.

"You really can't?" Frankie asked in a small voice.

Zora shook her head. She couldn't make a drawing for Frankie's birthday, and riding lessons from Grandma Wren seemed like a long shot. What if Frankie didn't get *anything* she asked for this year?

Zora couldn't let that happen.

Somehow, she had to make Frankie a picture of a horse. Zora crawled to the cast-off sketchbook and pencil, which had landed next to Frankie's *Horse Sense* book. She stared at the horse on the cover for a second, wondering. She couldn't *draw* Frankie a horse, but what if...

What if she *traced* one?

Zora opened the book to a photo of a big, brawny Shire horse. She laid a piece of blank paper over it. *Don't draw, just trace*, she told herself. She held her breath as she picked up the purple pencil, waiting for the panic to engulf her. But it didn't. The pencil lead glided over the curves and straights of the horse's body, following the lines beneath the paper. Zora exhaled. Tracing didn't feel fizzy and great like drawing with Voom, but it didn't make her feel like she was going to faint or throw up either.

She just felt...nothing. Numb.

Zora handed Frankie the finished tracing, and Frankie squealed. "Your Voom came back! I knew it would."

Zora said nothing. She watched Frankie tape the traced, fake, Voomless horse to the wall, right next to the drawing of the blue horse.

There was a knock on the bedroom door. "Girls, you can come out now!"

With Zora right behind her, Frankie tiptoed into Grandma Wren's kitchen like she was expecting a crowd of clowns holding balloons to jump out and yell, *Surprise!*

There were no clowns. No balloons. There was just Grandma Wren, who was wearing the gray bus driver uniform she wore every day and the heavy, black shoes that reminded Zora of Frankenstein. Her glasses had huge, square frames that seemed to cover half her face.

"Happy birthday!" Grandma Wren said. Zora scanned the kitchen for any sign that this was a party. Not even one streamer? Not a single balloon?

If Mom were throwing this party, the ceiling would be jam-packed with balloons, their ribbons hanging down like jungle vines. Streamers would be strewn about as if the room had been TP'd by teenagers. Mom would kazoo the heck out of "Happy Birthday" as she danced around the kitchen. There'd be a homemade cake that looked like it belonged in an art museum.

Now, Zora's eyes landed on a lopsided cake on the kitchen table. White frosting was smeared unevenly on the sides, like sunblock lotion applied in a rush. On the top, drawn in thick blue frosting that resembled toothpaste, was a picture of... something.

Frankie stiffened when she saw the cake, the way you might if you spotted a nest of snakes.

"It's a horse!" Grandma Wren said, gesturing to the cake. "See, here's the head and then...well...you get the idea. I'm no artist. I should've asked Zora to draw it."

I wouldn't have been any help, Zora thought.

"How about some party music?" Grandma Wren said. She fiddled with the radio by the fridge, tuning into the jazz station. Zora hated jazz. The notes sounded mixed up and lost, like they had wandered into the wrong song.

Grandma Wren turned to face the girls, her hands on her hips. "What should we do first? Cake or presents?"

Frankie's eyes darted to the scary cake and then back to Grandma Wren. "Presents," she blurted.

"You got it." As Grandma Wren reached for an envelope on the counter, Frankie shot Zora a gleeful look. *Riding lessons!* Zora's heart bobbed into her throat. Maybe Grandma Wren had decided to give Frankie the lessons after all. Maybe she realized what a big deal it was to Frankie.

Grandma Wren handed the plain white envelope to Frankie, who tore into it. She pulled out two small plastic cards. Frankie examined the colorful fronts and then the backs, each of which had a black stripe down the side. She looked up. "Are these tickets to my riding lessons?"

"No," Grandma Wren said. "I thought of something even *more* fun than riding horses."

Frankie's face grew suspicious. There was nothing more fun than riding horses.

"Those are bus passes," Grandma Wren said. "I'm taking the day off tomorrow, and my boss is letting me borrow a bus. I'm gonna drive you girls on your own personal tour of Pittsburgh, so you can get to know your new city."

Frankie gasped. It was her *oh-no* gasp, but Grandma Wren

must've heard it as *oh wow*, because she smiled. "I know! A whole bus, just for us. *That* is your birthday present!"

Frankie's eyebrows formed a pointy roof over her eyes, which were flooding from the basement. "But...Mom promised."

Blood thundered past Zora's ears. First she gets a stupid traced horse from Zora and then stupid *bus passes*? Frankie deserved better than this on her birthday.

Grandma Wren rubbed her chin. "I know, Frankie. But I'm not sure horseback riding is safe for a kid your age."

Silent tears spilled down Frankie's cheeks. No riding lessons, and Grandma Wren had called her a kid. Zora knew how much she hated that.

"Listen, Frankie," Grandma Wren said, sinking candles into the horrible cake. "The bus ride will knock your socks off. I promise. Okay?"

Frankie attempted a smile and gave a small nod. Zora's face flamed. Hadn't Frankie dealt with enough empty promises for one day?

"And Zora," Grandma Wren said, "I know it's Frankie's birthday, but I wanted you to have something to open too."

She pushed a slim package wrapped in tissue paper across the table. Zora didn't reach for it. *I don't want a present.*

"Open it," Frankie demanded.

Zora tore the white tissue paper, revealing an ancient-looking spiral notebook. Written in a childish cursive on the faded brown cover was *Nina Webb.* Mom's name.

Zora thumbed the corner of the pages like a flip-book. All the pages were blank. Except no—there was one drawing on the first page. A little girl running in a field of flowers.

"I found it in your mom's old things, from when she was a kid. Nina must've filled a hundred sketchbooks, but she never finished that one." Grandma Wren turned the book to a clean page. "I thought you could use the paper."

Zora clenched her jaw. "No. I can't."

"Of *course* you can. You mom would be happy you're using her old sketchbook. She was so proud that you're an artist, Zora. You'll always share that connection with her."

The words were like a punch in the gut. Zora *didn't* share that connection with Mom anymore. She stared at the empty sketchbook page. It looked blanker and blanker by the second, like the whiteness was a bottomless pit that she was falling into.

"Happy birthday to you..."

As Grandma Wren sang, Zora's ears rang with the total lack of kazoo. What was happy about this birthday or any other day from now on? Mom wasn't here. If Zora hadn't drawn that brutally truthful picture of her in the hospital and forced Mom to face how sick she was, maybe she wouldn't have died that night. If Zora had drawn her strong and healthy like Mom asked her to, maybe she would've gotten better. She would be here now, kazooing and dancing and giving Frankie the birthday present she deserved.

It was all Zora's fault.

Tears tightened her throat, choking her. A heavy darkness snowballed in her chest. Zora shoved away from the table, knocking over her chair. She raced down the hall to her bedroom and slammed the door.

Zora stormed over to the traced purple horse taped above Frankie's bed. Also known as the Worst Birthday Gift Ever. She yanked the pitiful picture off the wall. She grabbed her pencil tin from the nightstand and threw off the lid. She chose a dark-green pencil, and the familiar wave of hot panic crashed over her. But then...

A different feeling rose up, pushing the panic aside. A murky, roiling tornado spiraled down her arm and into the pencil. Zora attacked the purple horse with heavy green scribbles.

Frankie burst through the bedroom door. "Hey! Stop ruining my birthday present!"

"It was ruined to begin with." Zora covered the horse's eyes with dark-green spirals. She scribbled zigzags over its mouth, giving the horse two green fangs as long and sharp as daggers.

"But the Voom came back," Frankie pleaded.

"No, it didn't. I *traced* this. Tracing isn't the same as drawing," Zora said, her pencil picking up speed. The horse's graceful mane and tail became snarled nests that seemed to twist and writhe on the paper.

It wasn't the bright, fizzy feeling of Voom or the numbness of tracing. The energy surging down her arm was slippery and dark, and it spread in her like an oil spill.

It felt *great*.

She was hungry to wreck more.

Zora's eyes traveled up the tower of moving boxes, which had sat unopened for months. The box on the very top held all of Zora's old sketchbooks and the framed drawings from the dining room. She hadn't wanted to open the box, knowing that the drawings would only make her remember. Mom. Voom. Duluth. Everything she'd lost. But now, with a slippery cyclone spinning in her chest and armed with a pencil, Zora wasn't afraid.

She stormed over to the stack of boxes. Grandma Wren wanted her to unpack them? Oh, she'd unpack alright. Zora jerked the box on top to the floor.

"Careful!" Frankie cried. "That's the Permanent Collection."

Permanent? No such thing. Zora ripped off the tape and slapped open the cardboard flaps. Shards of glass covered a drawing of a panda with monkey hands and feet.

Frankie gasped. "You broke the glass."

"Good." Zora tweezed the panda picture out from under the shards, and the memory of drawing it sliced into her. The Duluth Zoo a few winters ago. While they all stood around the monkey exhibit, Mom said, "What if a panda and a monkey had a baby?" Zora drew the monkey-panda, and Mom thought it was so adorable that she hugged it to her chest, then pressed it to the glass so the monkeys could see it too.

Tears stung Zora's eyes as she covered both the monkey-panda and the memory it held with thick scribbles the color of swamp water. Her pencil slid across the paper with an ease she

41

hadn't felt for months. So the Voom wasn't ever coming back? *Good.* She wished there never was any Voom in the first place. She wished she had never drawn anything.

"Stop it!" Frankie tried to wrench the pencil out of Zora's hand. Zora elbowed her away. Frankie ran into the hall.

Zora yanked a sketchbook from the box. She flipped to a page full of dinosaur skeletons. The memory of drawing them trampled her. Their last camping trip to the Boundary Waters. By the fire before bedtime, Mom said there were probably dinosaur fossils directly beneath their folding camp chairs, deep underground. Zora drew by flickering firelight while Mom and Frankie made s'mores.

No! Zora buried both the dinosaur skeletons and the memory under dark-green scribbles. She flipped to the next page and the next, destroying picture after picture. A narwhal with wiener-dog legs. A

42

lion with a dragon's tail. So many horses. The pictures vibrated with memories of when and where Zora drew them. *The kitchen table after dinner. The bus ride home from school. Mom's big, warm bed on a Saturday morning.* Each memory was like a paper cut going deeper and deeper.

Zora's pencil raced even faster now, her hand shaking as she tried to keep up. The thick, green scribbles seemed to tremble too. She would destroy every last drawing, until there were no more reminders of their old life. Outside the bedroom window, the sunset stained the sky a murderous red.

"Zora." Grandma Wren stood in the doorway with a wide-eyed Frankie, who had apparently gone to get her. Tattletale. "What's wrong?"

"Everything!" Zora yelled. Mom was dead, and from now on they had to live with a grandmother who gave them bus rides and ugly cake for their birthdays in a lakeless city in an underground apartment that sounded like jazz and smelled like a rummage sale, one they could never leave.

Grandma Wren took a step into the room. "Remember, Zora—"

"No!" Zora shouted. "I'm sick of remembering."

Grandma Wren held up both hands. "I'll give you some space," she said, then gently closed the door.

"She was just trying to help," Frankie said in a wobbly voice.

"I don't want her help." Zora dug to the bottom of the moving box and tugged out a stack of construction paper. She riffled through the drawings she had made when she was little—houses and clouds and trees and dogs—then flung the stack across the floor like a Frisbee. Frankie scrambled to rescue a Halloween witch and a horse with a body like a hotdog. Zora grabbed another sketchbook from the box and wrenched the pages from the spiral binding with a strength she didn't know she had. She chucked the drawings to the floor.

Zora kneeled on the wide scattering of pictures. Gripping her dark-green pencil like a dagger, she scrawled one giant scribble across the whole mess of drawings. Her head swam with the slick, scribbly feeling.

"Why are you doing this?" Frankie's voice was wet with tears.

"You're too little to understand."

"I'm not little," Frankie growled. "I just turned *seven*."

"Pff," said Zora. Didn't Frankie get it? She could turn

44

seven or seventeen or seventy and their lives would still be over. The friction of the pencil burned Zora's fingertips. The scribble lines at the edge of her vision squirmed and swelled.

"You used to be nice," Frankie said. "We used to have *fun*. Now you're just mean!"

"That's right."

As Zora made the scribble spot bigger and darker, the darkness expanded in her too.

I will never draw anything ever again, she thought.

Zora leaned so hard on the pencil, it snapped in half with a loud crack.

Frankie yelped like a dog that had been kicked. Mom had bought Zora that set of pencils at the Paint Box, a professional art store, for her eleventh birthday. They were so special, Zora had waited a whole week before she started using them.

Zora stared at the broken green pencil, one piece in each hand like the halves of a wishbone.

"Ooooh, I broke a pencil," Zora said. "Big deal." Just one more thing that was broken and couldn't be fixed.

Zora stood and shoved a pencil half into each of her hip pockets, like a cowgirl holstering her guns.

"Your drawings," Frankie whispered, staring at the floor.

"Forget them. They're dead."

A loud, scratchy noise surged behind Zora, and she turned toward it. Two dark-green lines rose up from the pile of scribbled papers like a pair of charmed snakes. The lines swelled, becoming thick ropes. A pungent, smoky smell hit the back of Zora's throat.

Zora's heartbeat quickened as time slowed. Her mind scrambled to make sense of what she was seeing.

The ends of the two scribble ropes stretched tall, until they almost touched the ceiling. They swiveled side to side, like they were looking for something.

"Wh-what are those things?" Frankie asked.

Before Zora could say *I have no idea*, one of the scribble ropes darted down at Frankie, like a viper striking. Frankie stumbled back, her bunk bed catching her behind the knees.

Zora leapt between her sister and the burly rope, whacking it with the back of her hand. "Stay away from her!"

The green rope hit the wall with a meaty thud, quickly recovered, and then dove for Zora. It caught Zora's wrist in a winding grip. Whatever these things were, they weren't friendly.

The other scribble rope wound itself around Frankie's ankle. She grabbed fistfuls of the bedsheet as the rope dragged her to the floor. "Zora, help!"

Zora's rope whipped her up high, her hair almost snagging in the whirring blades of the ceiling fan. Frankie's scribble rope reared back and flung her up high too.

Frankie and Zora hovered, suspended, everything still like at the top of a roller coaster. Zora and Frankie shared a wide-eyed look. *Was this actually happening?*

Then the space between them stretched like a rubber band. Frankie zoomed way, way out of Zora's reach, becoming as tiny as a toy action figure in her cutoff jeans and T-shirt. The ceiling fan expanded until its blades were as broad as airplane wings. The walls pulled back and the room grew wide and tall around them. The bunk beds and bureau towered like skyscrapers.

The floor now seemed miles away, everything miniature and hazy—the way the ground must look to a skydiver right before the big jump out of the plane.

Zora's mind flailed, trying to understand what was happening. Her heart banged against her ribs like it desperately wanted out. Her eyes traveled down the dark-green rope that had captured her by the wrist, all the way to the far end of it. It was like the world's longest electrical cord, plugged into what seemed like acres of scribbled papers on the broad expanse of braided rug far below. Frankie's rope was also plugged into the paper.

From that incredible height, they fell.

A jagged scream ripped from Zora's throat, but the air blasting past her ears swallowed the sound. She starfished her arms and legs, the wind plastering her sweatshirt and shorts against her skin. Loose fabric snapped on the sides of her body. Even though she was wearing socks and tennis shoes, cold air shot between her toes.

Fifty feet away, Frankie hurtled headfirst toward the field of scribbled drawings below, the green rope trailing like a comet tail from her ankle. Frankie was going to go splat. Zora too.

They were going to die.

Zora fought the wind resistance to turn her head toward Frankie. Still rocketing downward, Frankie was somehow moving closer to Zora, until she was just out of arm's reach.

"Frankie!" Zora yelled into the deafening roar.

She stretched her fingers toward her little sister, whose mouth was stretched wide in a scream. If she could just catch hold of Frankie, maybe she could get underneath her to break Frankie's fall.

Frankie pointed at the ground. Zora snapped her attention to the paper-covered ground, which was now only thirty, twenty, ten feet away and sucking in the last of their scribble ropes. "No!" Zora cried, thrusting her hands out in front of her.

RRRRRRRRIP!

Zora's palms plunged through the paper.

5

Ow.

Zora's entire body throbbed, like a funny-bone feeling, except all over. She opened her eyes. An incredibly bright light forced them shut again.

She coughed out a mouthful of—what was this stuff? She ran the tiny, spongy balls between her fingertips. The balls were nearly weightless, like the Styrofoam inside a beanbag chair.

Zora fought the painful light with her eyelids, finally

managing to slit them open. *Am I dead?* she wondered. *Is this that tunnel of light you always hear about?*

Zora pressed her hands down to sit up, and the soft, loose ground shifted beneath her. She didn't *feel* dead. Gradually, her eyes adjusted to the brightness. She looked down at the tiny orange, yellow, and brown dots surrounding her. It was like she was in a ball pit, but she was giant compared with the balls. This wasn't the pile of scribbled papers she had been falling toward. It appeared to be a beach.

But...a beach made of Styrofoam sand?

She examined her wrist, chafed from where the scribble rope had clutched her tight. But the rope itself was gone.

A cool breeze tickled the nape of Zora's neck. She turned, shielding her eyes with her hand. Flat, overlapping layers of turquoise and cobalt and sapphire and cerulean and indigo and every other imaginable shade of blue slid up and down, all the way to the horizon.

Zora squinted. Was it a lake? Kind of, though not any lake Zora had ever seen before. Some of the blue layers had the grainy look of crayons on construction paper. Some had the soft bleed of watercolors. Some seemed to be made with colored pencil, and a few had what looked like giant finger lines combing through glossy paint. The layers rose and fell softly, like the water was breathing.

"Zora?" said a muffled voice.

Frankie. Zora remembered her sister with a jolt. "Where are you?"

A small hand broke through the surface of the Styrofoam sand a few yards off. It gave a weak wave.

"I'm coming!" Zora crawled toward the spot where Frankie was buried, her hands and knees leaving dents in the loose, shifting sand. Zora grabbed Frankie's hand and pulled.

Frankie emerged, the foam sand rolling off her like water droplets off a duck.

"Are you okay?" Zora brushed dots out of Frankie's hair.

"Yeah." Frankie tried to open her eyes, then shut them with a grimace. "Whoa, it's so bright."

Zora squeezed along the length of Frankie's legs, checking for breaks. She seemed to be in one piece. The rope that had gripped her ankle was nowhere to be seen.

"Does anything hurt?"

"No," Frankie said. Then she gasped, like she had just

remembered something. "Zora, we fell!" Frankie collapsed back onto the soft sand with a *poof* and made a snow angel. A sand angel. "There were these *Jack-and-the-Beanstalk* vines and they carried us up and the room got all weirdly big and then we were falling like whoooooaaaaa and I was screaming and it was *so fun!*"

"Fun?" Zora raised an eyebrow. Almost dying wasn't fun.

A turquoise wave rushed toward the beach, where it crashed with the sound of crumpling paper. Zora's breath snagged in her throat. Wait. The water didn't just *look* like it was crayoned and penciled and painted. It *was* crayoned and penciled and painted.

Zora shaded her eyes and looked up. No wonder the light was so intense. Five suns, each one a different kind of yellow or orange, huddled together in the pale-blue sky. The suns' thick, stubbly rays looked like they were drawn with chunky baby crayons. The smallest orange sun suddenly broke from the pack and scuttled like a spider on its rays to the far side of the sky. The other suns chased it around in circles until a large yellow sun touched the small orange one with a long, golden ray.

"They're playing tag!" Frankie said, laughing.

Suns playing tag? A possibility dropped into Zora's head, making it whirl. The suns and the lake were drawings. Were she and Frankie also drawings? Zora quickly checked her palms, then the backs of her hands. Phew—normal. Frankie looked normal too. They weren't drawings, and they weren't dead. But—where were they? What was this place?

"Zora, look!"

Zora followed Frankie's pointing finger to the massive structure sitting on the grass that bordered the beach. The wheel was at least ten stories tall and drawn in black colored pencil. The capsule-shaped cars dangling from the edge of the wheel, swaying gently in the lake breeze, were red, blue, green, and yellow. Zora blinked. This wasn't just any Ferris wheel. It was the one from the Minnesota State Fair. A memory flooded her.

Sketching the wheel while Mom and Frankie waited in line for a bucket of french fries. The three of them soaring high above the fair on the wheel, eating the hot, greasy fries till they were stuffed, cheering every time their car reached the very top...

Zora squeezed her eyes closed and pushed away the memory.

"Come on!" Frankie said and took off running toward the wheel.

"*Wait*," Zora said, running after her. But Frankie was already climbing into the yellow car swaying at the bottom of the wheel. Worse, the giant wheel was starting to turn.

"Quick, jump in!" Frankie said.

Zora had no choice. She jumped in.

6

The Ferris wheel lifted their car, which made Zora's stomach drop and made Frankie squeal with delight. The shoreline grew small, and the view stretched wide. A series of rolling green hills led away from the beach where they had landed and ended in a large cluster of buildings—it looked like a city center. In the distance, Zora spotted a dense forest that merged with a hazy mountain range drawn in soft grays and purples. The whole place seemed to be surrounded by blue water. They were on an island...of drawings and paintings?

"Where *are* we?" Zora said.

"Pencilvania," said a voice. It was coming from the yellow car directly in front of them.

"This can't be Pennsylvania," Zora said. "We live in Pennsylvania, and it's nothing like—"

"*Pencil*vania." A face with whiskers and pointy ears peeked over the edge of the car. "You know, like the drawing tool?"

"There are talking cats here?" Frankie said. "I love this place already."

The cat blinked its large green eyes. "Everything she's ever drawn or painted is here."

Who was "she"? Zora had a sinking feeling.

"We're almost at the top!" Frankie announced.

"Then hang on tight," said the cat. "The ride's about to begin."

Zora frowned. "Aren't we already on a—"

A loud bang came from the base of the Ferris wheel, making the whole structure shudder. With a metallic screech, the wheel broke free of its base and began to roll. Zora flung an arm protectively over Frankie's lap.

As the Ferris wheel rolled up a steep green hill, the car holding Zora and Frankie descended, swaying wildly. When the wheel reached the top of the hill, their car was at the very bottom, near the ground, and everything went still. Zora reached for the door of the car, more than ready to get off this horrible ride, when the wheel began rolling again, faster and faster, speeding down what felt like the first big drop of a roller coaster. Zora's stomach flew into her throat.

"Wheeee!" said Frankie.

"Aaaaagh!" said Zora.

The wheel climbed another hill, then roared down the other side. The cars on the Ferris wheel circled wildly, churning Zora's insides. She lost count of how many hills, how many revolutions.

"Make it stop," Zora gasped.

"Can't stop!" said the cat. "Or else we'll be late."

"Late for what?" Frankie asked.

"For that," said the cat, pointing a paw at a bunch of brightly colored orbs bobbing above a grassy field. "The balloon release ceremony is about to begin."

The Ferris wheel sped down one last hill, then slowed as it crossed the wide, flat field. To the left of the field, the lake (or ocean?) stretched as far as Zora could see.

"Balloons for my birthday!" Frankie said, clapping.

The hundreds of balloons had chunky outlines, unmistakably drawn with broad markers. Each balloon had a string, and holding each string was a small, furry creature standing on its hind legs. But what kind of creature? Zora leaned forward to squint, then she pulled back. Hamsters wearing pajamas.

Those are my drawings.

The truth clanged in Zora's head like a loud bell. The hamsters were straight out of the slumber party scene that used to hang in the Permanent Collection. She had drawn the hammies in jammies when she was trying to convince Mom to buy her a pet hamster. *Okay, okay,* Mom said, relenting. *You're killing me with the cuteness.*

Zora squeezed her hands into fists until Mom's voice faded.

The Ferris wheel slowed by the edge of the field. Frankie scrambled out of the car and onto the grass, and Zora followed. The vibrant green blades were drawn in fat crayon and crunched underfoot. Zora was bending over for a closer look at the grass when something bumped her from behind.

"Excuse me," said a crayoned girl with hair that looked like bedsprings. She had just gotten off a car of the Ferris wheel,

which Zora had assumed was empty except for the cat. But now she saw that every car had riders, and they were all getting off. A drawing of a dog dressed like Santa. A skeleton holding hands with a stick person. A walking bouquet of broccoli. The crowd of Ferris wheel riders hurried toward the throng of hamsters, sweeping Zora and Frankie along with them.

As the creatures jostled Zora, the memories of drawing them jostled her too. *School project on the skeletal system. That time Mom enlisted Zora to help Frankie eat more veggies. Doctor's waiting room.* A dizzy feeling coursed through Zora, threatening to knock her over.

The pj-wearing hamsters broke out in song.

Oooooooo, ooo
Praise her, praise her
Oooooooo, ooo
Her eyes shoot lasers

The hamsters swayed to the rhythm of their song and clapped their paws, which made the balloons they were holding dance.

"Scooch up, I can't see!" yelled the broccoli stalk, waving everyone toward the hamsters with its lanky green arms. The crowd plowed Zora and Frankie closer to the singing hamsters.

Two hundred feet tall
She'll save us all
Let's tell her stories
And sing her glories

Frankie nudged Zora. "Is this a surprise party for my birthday?"

"Are you joking?" Zora said. This was a nightmare, not a party.

Frankie gave her a sly smile. "Don't worry. I'll act surprised."

Zora gaped at her. Did Frankie honestly think Zora was making all this happen? That she had brought them to this place on purpose, only seconds after she swore off drawing for good?

The breeze wafted a fruity perfume that Zora recognized right away. Scented markers. She used to love that smell. Zora pulled the fabric of her sweatshirt over her nose. Every cell in her body screamed the same thing: Get me out of here!

"Attention, Pencilvanians!" someone squeaked. Zora and Frankie, along with the hushed audience of creatures, watched a chubby orange hamster wearing pink pajamas solemnly waddle forward with her blue balloon.

"We gather here today," said the hamster, "like every day, to celebrate our creator. To offer our gratitude for the magnificent world she has made!"

All of the hamsters raised their balloon strings high, like torches.

"She has laser gaze!" cried the orange hamster. "She has the power to make lakes laugh!"

"She is Zora!" shouted the crowd.

When she heard her name, Zora's stomach plummeted like an elevator with a cut cable. Now there was no denying it. They were definitely in a world of her drawings. *All* of her drawings, according to that cat on the Ferris wheel.

But if everything she ever drew was here, that included...

The drawing of Mom on her last night in the hospital. Mom at her sickest, Mom right before... Zora's insides coiled with guilt. Was she here now, in this crowd?

Frankie elbowed Zora. "These are your drawings, aren't they?"

Zora nodded weakly.

"And now they're alive?"

Another feeble nod.

Frankie broke into a huge smile. "This is the best birthday ever."

"Zora!" the orange hamster called out, and Zora held her breath. Had she been spotted? "Zora!" the hamster shouted at the sky. "We thank you!"

Phew—the hamster didn't seem to know she was here. *Let's keep it that way*, Zora thought.

"This is a party for *you*?" Frankie scowled. "It's *my* birthday."

Zora bugged her eyes at Frankie. Did she *ask* for a party hosted by her old drawings? Did she *want* to be in a place crammed with her artwork, which reminded her of everything she didn't want to remember?

"At first, everything was blank!" the orange hamster shouted, and the crowd fell silent. "At first there was nothing, then there was a girl named Zora. Zora made a dot, then a line, then a circle, then more dots and lines and circles to fill up the blank. And all that dotting and lining and circling made her hungry.

"Some of the circles became clouds. Some became lakes. And some became balloons, bright and juicy. Zora ate a balloon. And another. And more and more!"

On the makeshift grass stage, a black hamster in yellow jammies acted out the Zora part. It stuffed invisible balloons into its cheek pouches.

"Ha ha," Frankie said in singsong. "They think you eat balloo-oons."

"Shh," Zora said.

"The more balloons Zora gobbled, the bigger she grew," boomed the orange hamster. The black hamster climbed onto the shoulders of a gray one. "Her legs stretched as long as tree trunks. Her face grew to the size of the biggest sun. Her head grazed the clouds!"

A tower ten hamsters high wobbled and wavered. The top hamster gobbled imaginary balloons.

"Zora was fifty feet tall, then one hundred feet tall, then two hundred feet tall!" cried the orange hamster.

Zora pressed her hand to her head, which felt like it was filling with helium. Every time the hamster said her name, she felt closer to going *pop*.

Frankie crossed her arms. "No fair—you get to be two hundred feet tall. How come I'm not in this story?"

"Because you're lucky?" Zora said.

"They think you're so great," Frankie said, "but what if they knew you wanted to scribble them all out? And what if they knew you were here *right now*?"

Zora imagined hundreds of angry hamsters rushing at her and Frankie, baring their tiny, sharp teeth. "Frankie, don't you dare."

Frankie's face clouded over, but she didn't say anything.

"Zora," cried the orange hamster, "please accept these balloons, your very favorite food, as a token of our devotion. We hope that one day you will come to walk among us!"

"For Zora!" the hamsters chorused, releasing their balloons all at once. The crowd cheered. The candy-colored orbs soared up and out over the water.

Zora grabbed Frankie's arm. "Let's get out of here before anyone sees us."

"Stop bossing me, Zora."

"*Don't say my name.* They can't know I'm here."

"Let me *go!*" Frankie jerked free of Zora's grasp and tapped a tan hamster on the back. "Guess what? That's Zora." Frankie jabbed a finger in Zora's direction. "Right there. See? She's not two hundred feet tall."

The hamster let out an excited yelp and scurried away.

Zora's throat went bone-dry. "Not a good move, Frankie."

"*So-rry,*" Frankie sang with a devilish grin.

"Zora's here? *The* Zora? OMZ!"

Her name bubbled through the crowd like soup coming to a boil. An itchy heat crept up Zora's neck. Hamsters and other creatures pressed in on Zora and Frankie.

"Zora has come!"

"Where?"

"Over there!"

7

"There she is! Zora! She's finally come to Pencilvania!" shouted the crowd as they pressed in for a closer look.

A stumpy penguin with a top hat (art class at Bay View Elementary) knocked Zora into a green alien that stank of permanent marker (program for the fourth-grade musical). Something touched her back. Zora whirled to watch a turkey waddle by, its colorful tail shaped like a little kid's hand. *Her* hand. It was the Thanksgiving centerpiece from the year Mom made tacos instead of turkey.

Every time she collided with a drawing, she was hit with

another reminder of Mom and their old life, each one like a punch in the gut. Zora doubled over and clamped her eyes shut, but all that did was sharpen the smells of wax crayons and fruit-scented markers and sweaty fur. They had to get away from this crowd, from all these drawings, so Zora could actually *think*. So she could figure out how to get out of here.

The orange hamster in pj's ran up to Zora. "Is it really you?" she asked, gazing at Zora for a long moment. "It is!" The hamster threw itself at Zora's feet, paws outstretched. "You heard our call. You came!"

The rest of the hamsters bowed in Zora's direction.

"Whoa," Zora said. "I didn't hear any call, okay? We didn't come here on purpose."

The hamster sprang to its hind legs, eyes glistening with adoration. "Only someone as great as you would refuse to take credit. You're making yourself small to walk among us."

Zora shoved her hands into her hip pockets. Her fingers hit the two halves of the broken pencil she had pocketed back in her bedroom. In the confusion of the last half hour, Zora had forgotten they were there. When she touched the pencil shards, a prickly panic raced up her fingertips, into her arms, and filled her chest. Zora snatched her hands out of her pockets, and the frenzy in her body died down.

"I'm sorry we don't have any balloons for you to eat," said the hamster, wringing its paws. "We just let them all go."

"I don't eat balloons," Zora said. "They're for parties."

The hamster nodded. "Party food."

"Parties for growing two hundred feet tall," added a Halloween skeleton.

"*No*," Zora said. "Balloons are—never mind."

Frankie was laughing so hard, she could barely speak. "Why...why do you think she eats balloons?"

"I saw it with my own eyes!" said a dog wearing a polka-dot party hat. "Remember, Zora? You drew me holding a bunch of balloons. Then you put a balloon in your mouth."

In her mind's eye, Zora saw herself at the dining room table in their old house a few years ago, drawing a birthday card for Frankie. As she drew the dog in the pointy party hat, Frankie kept interrupting Zora by handing her balloons to blow up for the party.

"I wasn't eating them," Zora said. "I was blowing them up."

"Ah! Yes." The hamster nodded sagely. "So they'd be big

enough to eat. So you could grow two hundred feet tall, like the prophecy says."

"Prophecy?" Zora said.

A sound like distant thunder rumbled across the field. It grew louder. Closer.

"What's that noise?" Frankie asked.

Zora's heart drummed in her chest. "That sounds like..."

Hoofbeats. Dozens of horses galloped over the grassy rise at the far end of the field, hooves pounding, manes flying, heads nodding with the run.

"Horses!" Frankie threw her arms over her head like a game-show winner.

Some of the horses were crayoned and cartoony, with oval bodies and rectangle legs, running unevenly down the grassy slope. Some were drawn realistically from life, in pencil. Some were sketched with juicy markers and some were done in smeary oil crayon and a few were watercolor. There were horses with silky manes and curly manes; brown horses, green ones, gray, ruby red, yellow, chartreuse, turquoise...and they were getting closer by the second. So were the memories of where and why Zora drew them. *North Shore Stables. Mother's*

Day card. In line at the pharmacy. Doctor's waiting room. Each memory felt like leaning on a bruise.

"I'm going to ride that one! No, that one!" Frankie yelled over the ruckus of the hoofbeats.

The horses slowed as they approached the crowd of hamsters and other creatures.

"Everyone choose a horse," announced the orange hamster. "Then we'll ride to have all-you-can-eat pancakes."

"A horse ride *and* pancakes?" Frankie said. "This place is the best!"

"We're not staying for pancakes," Zora said sharply. They were leaving *now*. "Follow me."

She led Frankie toward a gap in the crowd, past a stocky polar bear and a flock of odd-looking birds, dodging the memories erupting from the pictures. *Fifth-grade report on migration. Doodling in bed while Mom read out loud.* Seeing her old drawings on paper would be bad enough. But these were 3D, moving reminders of Mom and the life they all lost.

"Zora?" said a deep voice. Zora turned to face a gray horse. His sketchy pencil outline wavered a bit, like heat waves on hot asphalt. He smiled down at Zora, his long gray teeth

overlapping and crooked, like keys on a piano that had been
left out in the rain. The horse had too many legs—three in
front and four in back, with knees pointing both forward and
back. "It's so good to see you," said the horse. "My name is
Airrol."

Zora tried to shut the door on the memory of drawing the
horse, but those seven wild legs kicked it wide open.

It was a windy Saturday morning at North Shore Stables, high in the hills overlooking Lake Superior. Zora and Mom sat on a bench, sketchbooks open on their laps. Frankie squatted by the wooden fence and talked to a silvery-gray horse that was trying to eat grass in peace.

"We don't have to stay long if you're tired," Zora said.

"I'm okay," Mom said. "Ready to try drawing from real life?"

Zora nodded.

"So pick a horse, any horse."

Zora scanned the fenced field. Brown horses, white ones, black ones...then her eyes came back to the gray horse Frankie was talking to. "That one."

"Good," Mom said. "Now keep your eyes on the horse, and without looking down at your paper, draw it. It's called 'blind contour drawing.'"

"But if I don't look at the paper, I can't see what I'm drawing."

Mom laughed. "Exactly. You just have to trust that it's going to turn out."

"If you say so." Zora locked her eyes on the gray horse and

moved her pencil into position. Voom hula-hooped in her chest and spiraled down her arm. Zora's eyes traveled down the slope of the horse's neck, into the dip of its middle back, and up the curve of its rump. Zora moved her hand along the lines she saw, the pencil softly rasping on the paper.

"Draw what you actually see, not just what you *expect* to see," Mom said. "Even if your picture doesn't end up looking technically perfect, it will be perfectly truthful."

Zora moved her pencil to the top of the horse's neck or at least where she hoped it was on her paper. She stared at the horse's ears. Usually when she drew horse ears, she made triangles. But now as she really looked, she saw that they weren't exactly triangles. More like—spoons? Rounded at the base, and not sharply pointed at the top. She drew the spoony truth of the horse's ears.

"Nice!" Mom said.

Zora moved on to the eye, like a pool of dark oil. Then she drew the wobbly nostril. The horse sniffed the breeze and lifted his lip, revealing one, two, three... at least six long yellow teeth. Zora sketched them without looking at the paper. Was she even still *on* the paper?

"You got this," Mom said. "You're doing great."

It *felt* great. The Voom was going gangbusters. Now for the horse's legs. Zora moved her pencil way over to the right, where she guessed the rump ended. Her hand slid down the rear leg line, to the sudden angle of the knee. It was pointing backward. Horses have backward knees? She had never noticed that before. She followed the slope from the knee to the hoof, then drew the other rear leg, then the first front leg.

"*Hey, horse,*" Frankie sang from the fence. The horse shivered its mane.

"Oh no, it's moving," Zora said. "Frankie, stop singing."

"*Horse, did you know you can run as fast as a car?*" Frankie crooned. The horse turned away from Frankie.

"Frankie," Zora said. "Stop!"

"Just keep going," Mom said. "Draw the legs where they are now."

"But I'll be drawing on top of the legs I already drew."

"I know. That's okay."

So even though the legs were facing the opposite direction as before, Zora added all four of them beneath the horse's

81

body, never peeking at the paper. "This is gonna turn out so weird," she said.

"Trust me, it's great," Mom said. "You can look now."

Zora dropped her gaze to the paper, and a laugh-scream leapt from her throat. The horse's teeth were way too big, crammed and crooked in its mouth. The coat, instead of sleek, was shaggy with gray sketch lines. And the legs.

Oh, the legs.

Some of the knees bent backward and some bent forward and there were one, two, three...*seven* total. Zora shook with giggles.

"I dig this picture so much," Mom said. She pointed at the too-many legs. "See, some people would call this part a mistake, but to me, it's what makes the picture feel alive."

Zora studied the drawing. Mom was right. Even though the lines were all over the place, they were full of energy and wildly alive. Voom welled up in Zora and surged far out beyond her edges. In that moment, everything felt right. Even the horse's crooked, crowded teeth and his centipede legs.

Now, everything felt so, so wrong.

"Are you okay?" asked the seven-legged horse named Airrol. "Can I help?"

Zora shook her head. Nobody could help. She just needed to get out of here. But where was Frankie?

Zora spotted her standing in a clump of horses. "Which one should I ride?" Frankie said, clasping her hands under her chin. "So many good choices."

"Frankie, let's go," Zora said.

Frankie wasn't listening. "Oooh!" she shrieked and bolted toward a giant horse drawn in blue marker. It was at least twice as tall as her. A fancy curled mustache sat on the end of its nose. "You're my favorite horse Zora ever drew!" She hugged the horse's tremendous cobalt leg. "I choose you."

The blue horse smiled. "Well, I choose you too." Her voice was high and tinkly like bells. "Climb aboard."

Zora grabbed Frankie's elbow. "No." They weren't riding horses or having pancakes. "We're leaving."

"Don't leave," said the orange hamster. "You just got here."

"I haven't had a chance to ride a horse yet." Frankie's voice cracked. Her lower lip wobbled. "It's my birthday."

The memory of drawing the horse swept over Zora. Frankie calling out facts from *Horse Sense* and asking Mom about riding lessons. *Next year, baby,* Mom had sworn. Next year, which was this year. Today.

"If you say you must leave, Zora, then surely you must," said the orange hamster. "But perhaps after your sister has one brief birthday ride?"

Frankie made begging hands at Zora. If anything would

make up for getting bus passes instead of riding lessons for her birthday, this was it.

"One ride," Zora said, holding up a rigid finger. "*One.* Then we're outta here."

8

"Thankyouthankyouthankyou!" Frankie cried, jumping up and down. Zora hadn't seen Frankie this happy in months. Zora found herself grinning too.

"You have to hang on tight," Zora said. "This horse looks fast."

"I will, I will!"

Airrol swung his sketchy gray head close to Zora. "Dee Dee is the second-fastest horse in Pencilvania," he said. "But she's very gentle and safe."

Zora nodded. "Safe is good."

Frankie flung herself against the blue horse in an attempt to mount it. She slid down the side like wet paint.

"I'll give you a boost," Zora said and made her hands into a little stirrup for Frankie to step into. But before Frankie had the chance, something bumped them both from behind.

"The Scribs!" shouted the penguin wearing a top hat, waddling frantically past them. "They're coming!"

"Oh no," Airrol said quietly.

The crowd erupted into jostling and shouting. "Out of the way! Run! It's the Scribs!" Zora was knocked sideways by a stick figure, then stepped on by a manga-style girl whose large eyes were filled with fear.

Zora scrambled to her feet. "Frankie?" Her sister was nowhere to be seen.

Hamsters and horses and other creatures fled in all directions. A colossal dark-green thing—it looked like a giant hairball—raced toward the field with a scritchy-scratchy noise mixed with wild growls and howls.

"Frankie, where are you?" Zora cried.

"Jump on my back," Airrol said. "We have to make ourselves scarce."

"But my sister—"

"Hopefully she's already run to safety. If we don't run now, we'll be very sorry," Airrol said. "Please, Zora."

Zora spotted Frankie. She was about twenty feet away from Zora, hanging onto the leg of the blue horse, which was trying to run away. As the massive green tangle got closer, Zora saw that it wasn't just a hairball.

Inside the snarl of scribbles were dozens of growling, snapping creatures. A deer with fork antlers charged on burly legs. A lion made long, nimble leaps, its dragon tail thrashing the grass. A furious-looking narwhal ran on stumpy wiener-dog legs, its horn aimed forward like a spear. Horses and dinosaur skeletons whinnied and roared. All of their bodies were wound with thick, dark-green scribbles.

"Run, Frankie!" Zora yelled.

Frankie didn't hear her. She didn't seem to notice the mass of scribbles either. All of her attention was on trying to mount the blue horse.

A huge purple horse covered in green scribbles broke out of the pack. Sickly green spirals spun where its eyes should be. Two emerald fangs glinted in a brutal grin. The fanged horse raced toward Frankie and the blue horse, a snarled green mane bouncing on its sinewy neck.

Zora's stomach flooded with acid. It was the horse Zora had traced for Frankie's birthday, then attacked with furious scribbles.

The scribbled horse whipped its tangled tail skyward, letting loose a long rope the color of swamp water. The rope formed a lasso in the air, then fell over the blue horse. The scribbled horse jerked its tail back, tightening the loop around the blue horse's legs. The blue horse toppled to the ground. Frankie screamed.

Zora ran toward her sister. "I'm coming, Frankie!" Her shout came out as a broken whisper.

The fanged horse swung another scribble lasso into the air. Frankie saw it and ran. The horse threw the lasso, which dropped over Frankie's shoulders. The scribbled purple horse gave the rope a yank, tightening it around Frankie's torso and knocking her off-balance. Frankie fell hard, her face crumpling in pain.

"No!" Zora cried, sprinting toward her sister.

Fwooomp!

The ground shook as the enormous scribbled horse landed directly in Zora's path, blocking her way to Frankie. With no time to stop, Zora crashed into the horse's burly front legs. They were as solid as tree trunks and cold as ice.

"How dare you touch me!" The horse reared up, his humongous front hooves hovering over Zora like a tidal wave. Murky-green scribbles snaked up his purple thighs, neck, and torso. Zora scrambled back to get clear of his hooves. The horse landed and glared at her with his scribbled eyes.

"You dare to interfere with...wait a minute." His voice shifted from furious to friendly. "Zora, is that you?"

He stepped toward her, exhaling curls of smoke that smelled like rotten eggs. It made Zora's eyes sting, but she was too terrified to blink. Or speak.

"It *is* you. You came," said the horse. "Allow me to introduce myself. I am Viscardi." He tossed his tangled mane out of his face and grinned. "Since the moment you created me, I've been waiting for your arrival. You, the diva of demolition! The queen of cross out!"

His scribbled eyes spun like whirlpools, sucking Zora into their depths. "I will help you, as you use your pencil to scribble out all of Pencilvania. Together, we will bring this world down." Viscardi gave her a deep bow.

Zora slid both hands into her hip pockets and touched the two halves of the broken pencil. Her breathing tightened,

her vision swam, and the panic began closing in. There was no Voom and she couldn't draw and she couldn't breathe and Mom was gone and—then a cool, oily darkness spilled down Zora's arms. A dark, slippery feeling spread in her chest. She exhaled. Deep in her pockets, she rolled the pencils slowly against her thighs, remembering how the lead had skated so smoothly and easily across the paper as she scribbled out her drawings.

Viscardi stood. "Destroying things feels delicious. Doesn't it?"

Zora bit the inside of her cheek. It *had* felt good to bury her drawings under those fast, slippery lines.

"Stupid drawings with their stupid memories," Viscardi said, pooching out his lower lip. His eyes spun faster. "You of all people deserve some fun. Let me show you how *I* have a good time."

Zora watched Viscardi's hypnotic eyes turn and turn. She nodded. Yes. Fun. Good.

Viscardi whipped his tail, sending three scribble ropes high into the air. They formed into three lassos, which shot into the crowd trembling at the edge of the field. One by one the lassos arced back, each holding a creature. A hamster in pajamas. A stick figure. The dog dressed as Santa. Viscardi flicked the prisoners down into the pack of Scribs, which swallowed them up.

"Such a blast," Viscardi said. "Of course, with your pencil, we can have even *more* fun." He stepped to one side, revealing a small, dazed-looking girl on the grass. Zora blinked. Who was that?

Frankie.

Zora shook her head, clearing it of Viscardi's spell. She jerked her hands out of her pockets, away from the pencil shards and the slick, scribbly feeling. "That's my sister. Let her go."

Viscardi cocked his head. "Ah, yes. I see the resemblance."

"Let her go!"

"Why, because you want to scribble her out free-range?" Viscardi smiled. "In the *wild*. I like it."

"I don't want to scribble out my sister," Zora said. "I don't want to do *anything* in this place."

"Oh, really?" Viscardi narrowed his eyes. "And yet you came here. And I'd bet my left fang that you brought a pencil with you."

Zora reached into a hip pocket. The soothing scribbly feeling bloomed in her chest again. She pulled her hand from her pocket and held up the pencil half. The point was still sharp. "So what if I did?"

"SHE HAS BROUGHT A PENCIL!" Viscardi roared in triumph. The gang of Scribs cheered. Faint squeaks and whinnies of terror rose from the grassy ridges on either side of the field. Next to Zora, Airrol's piano-key teeth chattered out a terrified rhythm.

"You see, Pencilvanians?" Viscardi said. "The Destruction at Dawn prophecy is underway. As the prophecy says, 'Zora will come bearing a pencil. On the Blank Bluff at dawn, the pencil will end what must be ended'!" Viscardi jerked the scribble rope that bound Frankie. Frankie yelped in pain.

"No!" Zora shouted. "I didn't bring a pencil here on purpose. I don't know anything about your stupid prophecy. Release my sister NOW!"

Viscardi's upper lip curled. "I get the feeling you're not going to cooperate. I guess I'll have to wipe out the world by myself." He stepped toward her. "Pencil, please."

"Don't give it to him, Zora!" came a squeaky voice from the grassy ridge. "He'll use it to scribble out everything and everyone in Pencilvania!"

Zora made a tight fist around the pencil. Frankie was all that mattered.

"If I give it to you," Zora said, "you free my sister. Deal?"

"Of course," Viscardi said, his voice as light as a cloud. "I promise."

Zora held out the pencil. A rot-colored scribble rope shot from Viscardi's snarled mane. It wound around the pencil and jerked it from Zora's hand.

"Thank you, dear," Viscardi said with a sugary smile. His scribble rope tucked the pencil behind his ear, then he faced his gang. "Scribs! Grab the sister."

"No!" Zora cried, lunging for Frankie, but Viscardi blocked her. The lion with the dragon tail leapt from the pack of Scribs. It grabbed Frankie's scribble rope in its teeth and dragged a screaming, thrashing Frankie behind Viscardi.

"You promised you'd let her go!" Zora said.

"Promises break, darling. You of all people should know that." Viscardi smiled down at her, sunlight winking off his dark-green fangs. "I'm taking your sister so I can scribble her out first thing in the a.m."

"I wanna go home," Frankie sobbed.

"I wonder..." Viscardi said. "Will scribbling alone be enough to kill her? Or will I need to bite her? Or sit on her? I could squash her right now!" He lifted a massive hoof over Frankie's small, quivering body that was bound in scribble rope.

"Don't!"

"Right you are, Zora," Viscardi said, lowering his hoof to the sand. "The prophecy says that the destruction will begin at dawn, so I must wait till morning. But I do need to make sure the pencil works, so..."

"Stop him, Zora!" A small peach-colored hamster in green pajamas charged out into the open, its arms spread wide. "Grow to your true height! Blast him with your laser eyes!"

"Oh, shut up," said Viscardi. With two quick slashing motions, Viscardi drew an X over the creature. The hamster let out a sad squeak. Its body shriveled smaller, smaller then... it was gone.

All that was left was the dark-green X, which dropped to the grass with a soft thud. A collective cry of anguish erupted from the edges of the field.

Zora stood frozen, staring at the X. Viscardi killed the hamster. He was planning to do the same to Frankie.

"Oh, good, the pencil works," said Viscardi.

Zora flung herself at Viscardi now, grabbing hold of the scribbles covering his eyes. They buzzed with electricity under her palms. Viscardi roared in fury or pain or both. Zora reached for the pencil hovering just out of reach at the end of Viscardi's scribble rope.

"Get off!" Viscardi shouted, shaking her loose. One of his fangs sliced across her forearm, and she fell to the ground. Zora drew in a sharp breath against the searing pain.

"Sorry I can't stay and wrestle, Zora, but I must be off to prepare for the Destruction at Dawn." His eyes whirled like dirty water going down a drain. "Tomorrow morning, all of you have a date with *the pencil*."

Yelps and whimpers rose from the edges of the field.

Viscardi galloped off, his gang of Scribs following close behind. Frankie bounced limply on the lion-dragon's back, her legs dangling off the side like a rag doll.

Zora chased the wild, green tangle of Scribs off the field and over the crest of a hill. She was going to catch Viscardi and save Frankie.

She had to.

9

Zora chased the Scribs as they raced toward a dense cluster of tall narrow hills just ahead. There were maybe seven or eight hills total, and each was a different color—red and yellow and lavender. One had blue and white stripes. The tops of the hills were shrouded in thick white clouds.

Zora's legs and lungs burned as she ran harder and faster than she ever had in her entire life. But still, the distance between her and the Scribs grew.

Viscardi and his gang raced straight for the base of the hills as if they were going to crash into them. At the last moment, they narrowed their scribbly pack and flowed into a gap between two hills. Zora followed, her legs feeling like Jell-O.

She lost sight of the Scribs as they wove through the maze of those hills. She followed their growls and howls, but then she lost the sound too. It was drowned out by a rhythmic chant—Zora couldn't make out the words. When she finally found her way out of the maze and into the open, the Scribs were long gone. She dropped to her knees, her vision blurring with tears.

The sound of slowing hoofbeats came up behind her. "Zora," Airrol said. "Are you okay? Oh no—you're bleeding."

The wound from Viscardi's fang was no paper cut—it was deep. If she could get sliced and bleed, Viscardi could really hurt Frankie too. This wasn't pretend.

"Don't worry about me. It's Frankie who needs help," Zora said, squeezing the throbbing cut closed. "How did Viscardi take over so fast, anyway?" She had only traced him and scribbled him out a few hours ago. "He *just* got here."

Airrol sucked his teeth. "Viscardi has been in Pencilvania for weeks."

Zora heaved a huge sigh. Time was screwy here, just like everything else.

At the base of the hills was a small gathering of creatures—a gray wolf wearing a basketball uniform, a snowman with carrot horns, a half-finished drawing of a lemur, and some stick figures. They shook their fists, if they had them, or their stick arms. They continued the chant Zora hadn't been able to make out before.

Here's the truth, it's time to shout
Zora wants to cross us out

"Protesters," Airrol said, shaking his head. "There's more every day. Just ignore them."

103

Get it through your crayoned head

Zora really wants us dead

"Listen up, everyone: Viscardi has killed a hamster!" someone squawked. A large red bird with lopsided wings swooped overhead. "He killed her with the pencil Zora brought. She's here! The prophecies are true!"

A cry of outrage burst from the protesters. They pointed at Zora. "There she is!"

A black horse carrying a handful of hamsters on its back came to a stop near Zora. A mustard-colored horse rode up beside it. The broccoli stalk riding the yellow horse jumped to the ground.

"*You.*" The broccoli aimed a skinny green finger at Zora. "You just stood there as he scribbled that poor hamster to death."

"What was I supposed to do?" Zora asked.

"Oh, I don't know," said the broccoli. "Maybe *draw* something to stop him? Isn't that what you do?"

Zora slipped her hands into her pockets. One was empty. The other pocket had the remaining half of the broken pencil. When her fingertips touched it, the sleek, scribbly feeling seeped into them. The Zora who drew, who had Voom coursing through her body—she was a whole different person. Someone who didn't exist anymore. The only thing Zora could do with a pencil now was wreck things.

"It's just like the Destruction at Dawn prophecy says," said the basketball wolf. "You brought a pencil to destroy us all."

The hamsters gaped at Zora, crestfallen.

"I didn't bring it on purpose," Zora said. It was an accident. Wasn't it?

"You didn't just bring a pencil," said the red bird. "You *handed* it to Viscardi. Thanks to you, tomorrow morning all of Pencilvania is kaput."

"Traitor!" yelled the snowman with carrot horns.

"Now, now," Airrol said in a soothing tone. "There's no need for name calling."

"Zora wants to bring destruction to Pencilvania," said the basketball wolf. "Why else would she create Viscardi and the other scribbled creatures? And why would she give him the pencil?"

"There must be a good reason," said one of the hamsters. "A *noble* reason. Zora would never wish us dead."

"I was just trying to get Frankie back," Zora insisted.

"Yeah, and you were more than happy to trade all of us for her." The basketball wolf pounded a furry fist into his open palm.

Zora steeled her gaze. So what if she was? Hand still in her pocket, she felt the smooth, flat end of the pencil. Then she ran her thumb over the opposite end, jagged from where the pencil had snapped. If an angry mob came after her, she could sharpen the pencil and scribble everyone out.

The snowman started up a new chant.

Leave, Zora, go away
Leave now, don't delay

"I wish I *could* leave now!" Zora shouted. "But Viscardi has my sister, and I'm not leaving without her."

The hamsters stared at Zora, stricken, clutching their pajama-clad chests.

"Wake up and smell the crayons, Zora," said the broccoli. "Your sister is as good as dead now that Viscardi has a pencil."

"The tying-up-and-taking-prisoners business was bad enough," added the basketball wolf. "Now that Viscardi has a pencil, he can actually *kill* us."

"We're doomed!" wailed a small blue beetle.

"I'm sure your sister was a nice kid," said the broccoli. "But cut your losses and forget about her."

"Forget my sister?" Zora demanded. Blood slammed in Zora's ears like doors banging shut.

"Once Viscardi takes someone prisoner, there's zero chance of escape," said the red bird. "It's a one-way trip to his Lair of Despair. That place is crawling with guards."

"We must have faith!" cried a brown hamster in silver pajamas. "Surely this is all part of Zora's grand plan to *rescue* Pencilvania. Right?"

Zora's mouth hung open. Rescue Pencilvania? *Forget*

Pencilvania. If it were up to her, Pencilvania would never have existed to begin with. Frankie was the only one worth saving here.

"Let us remember another important prophecy," said a white hamster in blue pj's. "The Girl of One Million Ideas. It says, 'She will bring a million ideas to amaze us and save us.'"

"That's right! Of course!" cried the other hamsters.

"I don't have a million ideas," Zora said through clenched teeth. "I don't even have *one*."

"Oh no, the Great Zora is angry," said the white hamster. "Please, don't shoot us with your laser eyes!" It covered its face with trembling paws.

"I don't..." Zora stopped. What was the point of explaining that her eyes didn't shoot lasers? They all believed she ate balloons. They all thought she was secretly two hundred feet tall.

The snowman made a rude noise. "That's what I think."

"Now that everything is officially hopeless," growled the basketball wolf, "we might as well go eat pancakes. Come on, everyone, let's go have our last meal." He led the crowd away.

The hamsters followed on their black horse. "Hooray for pancakes!" they cheered. "Hooray for Zora!"

Zora leaned her back against one of the hills—the one with blue and white stripes. She felt her eyes welling up again.

"Zora?" said a voice, making her jump. It was Airrol.

"I thought everyone left," Zora said.

"Nope." Airrol gave her a shy smile that revealed a peek of his piano-key teeth, like a few high notes.

"I have to save Frankie, but I have no idea how to do it."

"Me neither." Airrol sucked his teeth. "You could ask the Zoracle."

"The what?"

"The Zoracle. They're very wise. They know just about everything about everything."

"I hope so," Zora said. "Where is this 'Zoracle'? Please don't say it's far away." Her legs still felt like Jell-O.

Airrol laughed. "Just look up."

10

Zora's eyes traveled up the side of the large blue-and-white striped hill. The top was covered in clouds. This was the Zoracle? A bunch of clouds?

"We have to wake them up first," Airrol said and pointed his nose skyward. "Zoracle, we seek your wisdom! Please awaken!"

The hills swelled wider. There was the sound of someone—or several someones—sucking in a deep breath. The clouds began to shift, revealing that the hills were topped with giant heads. Zora heads, to be exact.

They weren't hills at all. They were self-portraits. Ms.

Anderson, the school art teacher, had them do self-portraits every year since kindergarten.

Zora stared at her faces, which were all pursing their lips to blow the clouds away. Some of the faces were painted with crude, childish smears. Some were done in marker, with more skill. The biggest one, which wore a blue-and-white striped shirt, she'd drawn this past year in colored pencil. It actually

looked a lot like her. All of the self-portraits ended just below the shoulders, which were planted firmly in the ground.

"Whoa," Zora said under her breath.

"*We are awake*," the seven heads said in unison.

"Down here," Zora said, waving.

All of portraits' pupils shifted down to look at Zora. "*Zora is here. Just as we foretold*," they said.

"Viscardi kidnapped my sister," Zora called out. "I tried to stop him, but I couldn't. Airrol said you'd know what to do."

The Zoracle's seven heads nodded. "*Yes. You know what to do.*"

"No, I don't. That's why I'm asking *you.*"

"*Yes,*" the Zoracle said, "*you should always ask yourself.*"

Zora leaned toward Airrol, without taking her eyes off the gently smiling faces of the Zoracle. "You said these things were wise," she whispered.

"Very wise," Airrol said. "After all, they're the ones who brought us the prophecies."

Zora's heart deflated. What was wise about prophecies that said she had laser eyes and ate balloons?

"*When you ask yourself what to do, your self will answer,*" said the Zoracle.

"They're talking in circles," Zora said. "I just need a straight answer."

Airrol broke into a smile. "Aren't circles great? So round and friendly looking. Lines are good too, but circles—they're the best." Zora raised an eyebrow at him, and Airrol quickly added, "But if it's straight answers you want, it's best to ask very straight questions."

"I'll try." Zora squared her shoulders to the Zoracle. "My sister has been kidnapped by Viscardi and taken to his Lair of Despair. Can you go rescue her?"

"*No*," said the Zoracle.

"Why not?"

"*Because we don't have arms or legs. You didn't give us any.*"

"Touché," Zora said.

She snapped her fingers. "The prophecies! You're the ones who make those up. So can you make up a new prediction where Viscardi vanishes and my sister goes free?"

"*We do not make up the prophecies. They come into our heads and then we speak them.*"

"Yeah," Zora said slowly. "That's called 'making stuff up.'"

"*We will recite the prophecies for you, starting with the Destruction at Dawn. Then, the Girl with Laser Gaze. Then, She Who Makes Lakes Laugh—*"

"Uh-oh," Airrol whispered. "Once they start reciting, they can go for hours."

Zora held up both hands to the Zoracle. "Please stop. Listen: Is there anyone in Pencilvania who can rescue Frankie?"

"*Yes.*"

"Who?"

"*The one who can set things right is super strong, super smart, super* everything."

A memory shot through Zora like lightning: *Mom telling them about her disease at the all-you-can-eat pancake restaurant in Duluth.* Zora had drawn Mom with muscles, tights, and a cape. A superhero capable of punching out the villainous Leukemia.

Pow!

Relief washed over Zora. Super Mom was in Pencilvania. She could rescue Frankie. She could punch Viscardi into next Tuesday.

Zora addressed the seven heads. "Do you know where Super Mom is?"

"*We do not know of this 'Super Mom.'*"

"Maybe everyone calls her by her real name," Zora said. "It's Nina Webb." Tears sprang to her eyes when she said it.

The heads shook side to side. "*We do not know of this 'Nina Webb.'*"

"Describe her," Airrol suggested.

"She's got long, curly brown hair. She's wearing an orange-and-blue superhero costume. A cape and tights and knee-high boots."

"Yes. This one we know."

"Where is she?" Zora said.

All of the Zoracle's pupils shifted sharply to the right. *"She lives on the Blue Block."*

"I know where that is," Airrol said.

"You do?" Zora said. "Will you point me in the right direction?"

"Of course. It sits on top of that hill," Airrol said, tossing his head toward a large green swell.

"Thank you," she told him, then looked up at the Zoracle's faces. "And thank you."

"You're welcome." The seven heads bowed, closing their eyes. *"Now we will recite the prophecies, starting with the Destruction at Dawn. Then, the Girl with Laser Gaze..."*

Airrol leaned close to Zora's ear and whispered. "Let's go."

11

Zora hiked up the grassy hill, the lime-green blades making a crunching sound under her feet. As she climbed, the lakeshore came into view—layers of blue that ran all the way to the horizon. She heard soft hoofbeats behind her and turned.

"I can find my own way from here," she told Airrol. "Go have pancakes with the others."

The gray horse looked wistful. "I do love pancakes. And I *am* hungry."

"So go eat."

"I will, as soon as you find Super Mom." He tossed his long bangs out of his eyes. "Look, there's the Blue Block."

A large blue shape sat on the top of the hill, all sharp angles and edges. As Zora approached it, she made out windows with white trim. Bright-yellow doors. Redbrick chimneys. Pointy gray rooftops. Her breath snagged in her chest.

Some of the blue houses were the right size—the same as her old house in Duluth. Some were bigger, and some were the size of a dollhouse. A couple of the houses were drawn from the back, with the small porch and the two windows of Zora's and Frankie's bedrooms. Most of the houses showed the front, with its dandelion-colored door. The lines of the houses were created in everything from thick baby crayons to fine colored pencils by Zora at every age.

"Are you feeling ill?" Airrol asked. "You look as gray as me."

"It's just...that's my house." Or it used to be. She had lived there her whole life, until a few months ago.

"I understand. You want to go home." Airrol's lips rounded carefully around the word *home*, like a tiny planet.

Zora bit the inside of her cheek. Home? Grandma Wren's

apartment wasn't home. Neither was the blue house in Duluth—not anymore. Nowhere was home.

Zora looked up into the horse's eyes. "It's hard to explain—"

"No need to explain," the horse interrupted gently, his voice radiating kindness. "I'm just glad I got a chance to meet you before you go."

The clenched fist of Zora's heart relaxed a little. It's not like Pittsburgh was so great, but they had to go back. Where else could they go?

Zora walked more quickly toward the cluster of houses. Behind one of those yellow doors was Super Mom. She was the mom who always knew how to fix things and how to keep Frankie and Zora safe. She'd know exactly what to do. Zora lifted her fist to knock on the first door, then stopped. What if Sick Mom lived here too? The mom who was weak, who lied, who left them when Zora...she couldn't bear to finish the thought.

Zora swallowed hard and knocked.

The yellow door creaked open.

Standing in the doorway was...not Super Mom. Or Sick

Mom. The creature's body and head were all one piece—a lumpy oval drawn in thick black crayon, the size and shape of a large potato. It had black dots for eyes, a simple U-shaped smile, and arms and legs that were just straight lines—no hands or feet. Zora had no memory of drawing it, but she couldn't have been more than two or three when she did.

"Eeeee!" it cried, holding its arms out wide.

"That's not Super Mom," Zora said, backing away.

122

"No, it's an Eeep," said Airrol. "They were the first creatures to arrive in Pencilvania."

"Eeeeee!" the Eeep said again, and the other yellow doors
flew open. Zora scanned the doorways but didn't spot Super
Mom—or Sick Mom. Only potato people were peeking out,
blinking their dot eyes. When they noticed Zora, they cried,
"Eeeee!"

Airrol chuckled. "They're very excited you're here."

The Eeeps loped toward Zora with surprising speed con-
sidering none of them had knees. Zora caught herself smiling. She bit her lip to stop it.

"Are they friendly?" she asked.

"Oh yes," Airrol said. "Very."

One of the Eeeps lost its balance as it ran, maybe because
of the no-knee situation. Its lumpy body tumbled, arms and
legs flailing, bowling over two more Eeeps. The three creatures rolled toward Zora and Airrol.

As the crowd of approaching Eeeps thickened, more of
them tripped and fell and rolled, crashing into nearby Eeeps,
which also rolled, creating a tidal wave of potato people.
They rolled to a stop at Airrol's hooves and Zora's feet, one of

them bumping her shoe. Something Mom used to say flashed through Zora.

You were born to be an artist. Once you learned to hold a crayon, you and your Voom were unstoppable.

Zora jerked her foot away from the Eeep, as if she had touched a hot stove. She and the Voom *were* stoppable. So was Mom.

The fallen Eeeps waved their arms and legs in the air, like bugs marooned on their backs, smiling their permanent smiles.

"Poor things. Let's help them up," Airrol said, nudging one with his hoof.

"I don't want to touch them," Zora said. As she discovered at the balloon ceremony, touching the drawings made the memories intensify.

Airrol used the tip of his hoof to help an Eeep back onto its stick legs. The Eeep used its straight, elbowless arms like chopsticks to help another potato person stand. Both Eeeps lifted a stick arm and gave each other a high five. But since they had no hands or fingers—just stick arms—it was more like a high one. All around Zora, potato people helped each other stand, exchanged high ones, and turned to face Zora.

A giggle bubbled in the back of Zora's throat. "They're so...happy."

"That's their natural state, but they're extra jazzed at seeing you. Why wouldn't they be?" Airrol shifted his warm, liquid eyes to Zora and held her gaze. It made Zora fold and fold into herself, like origami.

The Eeeps opened their arms wide to Zora, jumping up and down on their stick legs. "Eeeeeee!"

"They're asking you for a group hug," Airrol said.

Zora shook her head. "I...can't touch them. Do they know where Super Mom is?"

"Tell them what she looks like," Airrol said, and Zora did.

One of the Eeeps lifted an arm. "Eeeee? Eeeeee."

"Really? Oh dear." Airrol's voice quavered.

"E-eeee, e-eeee, EEEEE!" cried another Eeep.

"No." Airrol lowered his head. "That's terrible."

"What are they saying?" Zora asked.

"She did live here. But a few days ago, Viscardi and the Scribs swept through and kidnapped her along with a handful of Eeeps."

Zora's shoulders sagged. "Just like Frankie."

"I'm afraid so," said Airrol. "The Scribs surely took her to Viscardi's Lair of Despair."

The Eeeps pointed their stick arms at a jagged, shaded purple mountain range in the distance. "*Eeeee*," they breathed.

The Zoracle had said that Super Mom was the only one who could set things right. If Zora could manage to free

Super Mom from Viscardi's prison, then Super Mom would take it from there.

"How do I get to Viscardi's lair from here?" Zora asked.

"Oh, now, Zora..." Airrol said, showing his bottom teeth. "It's too dangerous."

"Eeeeee!" cried the Eeeps, shaking their heads—which were their whole bodies—side to side.

"They're saying that you can't defeat Viscardi," Airrol said.

"I know I can't. But Super Mom can." Zora gazed toward the distant violet-colored mountains, where Viscardi's lair was. "If I can manage to free her, then she'll rescue Frankie and make sure we get out of Pencilvania in one piece."

Viscardi said he'd wait till tomorrow morning to begin his scribble spree, but what if he decided to start early? He had already proven that his promises were worthless. Frankie might be his first victim. Zora had to get to Viscardi's lair, fast. Nobody thought she should go, and nobody was going to help her. She'd have to go alone.

Zora strode in the direction of the purple mountain range.

"Wait, Zora." Airrol trotted after her on his jumble of legs.

"I'm going to Viscardi's lair, and you can't stop me."

"I'm not trying to stop you," Airrol said gently, and Zora turned to look at him. He blinked his long gray lashes. His eyes were huge and dark, but unlike Viscardi's eyes, they were kind.

"If you're determined to go, I want to help you." Airrol dipped his head close to Zora's. "Will you let me?"

Zora gave the smallest of nods.

"Good. Hop on," he said, positioning himself sideways.

Zora shifted her gaze to Airrol's seven legs. The Eeeps had no knees, and Airrol had too many. The knees faced every which way, making his legs look as swift as a handful of bendy straws. Could he even reach Viscardi's lair by dawn? There had to be a faster way to—

"Oh!" Zora said, clasping her hands. "Airplanes!" She had drawn tons of those. "Are there airplanes in Pencilvania?"

"Lots. You can usually find them Downtown, which is just over that next hill." He nodded at the grassy rise up ahead.

"*Great*," Zora said. An airplane would get them to Viscardi's lair so much faster than a horse with too many legs.

Maybe they'd even beat the Scribs there. And if Downtown was close, Zora didn't have to ride Airrol at all. They could walk. And soon, they'd fly.

Airrol and Zora plodded up the hill toward Downtown. The Eeeps stood in front of the many houses of the Blue Block, waving goodbye vigorously with their stick arms. When Zora raised a hand in farewell, the Eeeps cheered and gave each other gleeful high ones.

"How does everyone know who I am?" Zora asked.

Airrol flipped his bangs out of his eyes. "When you drew us, you saw us. Right?"

"Right." She had to look at the paper to see what she was drawing, except for Airrol, who she had drawn without even glancing at her sketchbook. But wait—she *had* looked at him when she added finishing touches to his eyes on the drive home from North Shore Stables. She had shaded them to appear 3D and liquid.

"Well," Airrol said, "as you looked at us, we looked back at you. Yours was the first face any of us ever saw. Everyone knows you created them, and they adore you for it."

In her mind's eye, Zora saw the angry protesters by the Zoracle. "Not *everybody* adores me."

"True," Airrol said. "But most of us do. And why wouldn't we? You drew the whole of Pencilvania. Every creature, every blade of grass..." He looked up at the uneven puffs of white drifting overhead. "You drew the clouds, probably when you were just figuring out how make circles. You drew the big lake that surrounds the whole of this land, you drew the Baby Lakes and all of our suns too. Every time you draw another sun, it gets brighter in Pencilvania. But that suits me fine. I love sunshine." Airrol beamed at her.

Zora's face grew hot. She wished he would stop giving her that look—like she was something special. She lowered her eyes to the grass.

There were thousands of little green lines on this hill alone. "There's no way I drew all of this grass," Zora said. "Or all that sand back on the beach?" The thought made her knees weak.

"Every grain of sand," Airrol said, nodding. "Every blade of grass. Think of all the dots and lines you've made in your life. Where would they go, if not here?"

"Uh, nowhere?"

Airrol laughed a horsey laugh. "Everything you draw or paint comes to Pencilvania."

Everything and every*one*. Sick Mom. If Zora ran into her, what would she say? Sorry? She *was* sorry, but she was also angry. And what kind of terrible person was mad at someone for dying, especially when it might've been her fault? Zora's stomach tightened around the questions, crumpling them into a ball.

Zora shaded her eyes against the bright sunlight, searching the sky for airplanes. There weren't any. But a large orange sun hung at a distance from a clump of maybe twenty other suns. The clump froze, then raced toward the orange sun, froze, and then raced. A small red sun finally caught up to the orange one, which twirled, its rays blurring like the spokes on a speeding bike wheel.

"They're playing Red Light, Green Light," Zora said. She and her old friends at Bay View Elementary used to play it at recess.

"Here we call it Sunlight, Funlight," Airrol said. "Of all the games, it's the suns' favorite."

Zora crossed her arms. "Things are so weird here. In the real world, there's only one sun, and it doesn't play games."

"Can you blame it?" Airrol said. "It's hard to play games by yourself. If there were more suns, they'd surely play together all day long." He trotted to the crest of the hill, and Zora followed.

From the top of the hill, Zora looked down at a wide, straight street lined with colorful buildings—some short, some tall. The skyscrapers drawn in chunky crayon leaned more than the ones drawn in colored pencil, and all of them were covered in small square windows. There were lots of houses too, with triangular roofs that pointed in all directions like party hats put on crooked.

When they reached the main street, Airrol's hooves made

a crisp *clip-clop* sound on the gray pavement. The pavement was covered in hatchmarks—a crisscross pattern Zora used to doodle on her school notebook covers. Memories leapt out at Zora as they passed a long white building (day trip with Mom and Frankie to the Minneapolis Institute of Art) and a log cabin with a spring of smoke coming out of the chimney (third-grade project on pioneers) and an orange-and-blue bounce castle—

"Zora, can you do this?" Mom was bouncing higher than any of the kids at the school carnival. She had all these moves: the 360-degree spin, the butt bounce, the air splits. Zora didn't know her mom was a secret trampoline genius.

Frankie went for the splits and ended up doing a back somersault instead. When she tried to stand up again, she couldn't—her knees were mush from laughing so hard. Watching Frankie shriek and collapse over and over made Mom and Zora so weak with laughter, soon they couldn't stand up either.

Zora took a sharp breath, jerking herself out of the memory. It felt like a million years ago that Mom was strong enough to jump in a bounce castle. It also felt like yesterday.

Zora looked up at a skyscraper with hundreds of tiny square

windows. Some of the squares had faces in them, which peered down at Zora. Most looked friendly or at least curious. But one of the faces scowled at Zora and whipped the curtains closed.

Airrol stopped. "If you want to catch an airplane, this is a good place. Although I must say, I don't know why—"

"Right here on the street?" Zora said.

"Yep." Airrol smiled his wonky piano-key smile. "They come by all the time. Just gotta be a little patient."

Zora leaned against the trunk of a tree, the solid pouf of leaves hovering over her like an enormous green cotton ball.

Clank, clank, clank!

Zora turned toward the loud metallic sound. A robot colored with silver and gold crayons glinted in the sunlight, marching toward them on stiff rectangular legs. Its arms were like long vacuum cleaner hoses ending in claw hands. Instead of a head, a large light bulb was screwed into the boxy torso, which was covered in silver and gold buttons.

"Hey, Sharley!" Airrol called out. "Look who's here."

The robot waved a claw hand at Zora, and his light bulb head blinked. "HOWDY." The voice seemed to come from the robot's chest.

Zora lifted her hand, more to block the oncoming memory than to say hello.

Christmas card for Mom, the year Mom said she wished Santa would bring her a robot to help her do laundry.

"Is that really Zora?" A warbly voice came from a red-orange building across the street. "Coco told me she was here and—oh my, it *is* her!" Slowly, a figure tottered out the open door. You couldn't really call it walking because the figure didn't have legs or feet. The body was one big black triangle— pointy at the neck and broad where it touched the ground. Its round green head had a bright-red smear for a mouth, like lipstick applied without a mirror. There were two dots for eyes, and the head was topped with a triangular black hat with a wide brim. Stick arms ended in circles with stick fingers. The witch tipped side to side, slowly making her way toward Zora and Airrol.

"I'm Hazel," the witch said. She took off her hat and bowed her completely bald head.

"Hi." Zora braced herself for the memory of drawing the witch. But it didn't come. Judging by the thickness of the crayon lines, she must've been really little when she drew it. Too young to remember. Hazel. Sharley. Airrol. She hadn't given them those names. So who did?

Hazel flipped her hat back onto her head. "You've grown since I last saw you, Zora. When you drew me, you were only yay big." She held her stick-fingered hand at the height of Zora's elbow. "Oh dear, you're bleeding!"

Zora had almost forgotten about Viscardi's cut on her arm. Now that Hazel mentioned it, it started to throb again. Hazel gingerly took Zora's hurt arm in her spiderlike hands. "Shar, go grab me a Band-Aid."

Sharley clink-clanked stiffly toward the red-orange

building. The wide front window was piled high with lamps and vases draped with bead necklaces and chairs and stuffed footstools and stacks of dishes and a watering can and a rack of clothes. It looked like a thrift store.

"Sharley and Hazel run the Everything Emporium," Airrol said. "It's a place to keep all the odds and ends you draw. They come in handy."

Hazel nodded, still cradling Zora's arm. "The Everything Emporium has everything except...*you know*." The witch made a yuck face. "Stuff to draw with. Markers. Crayons. Pe—pe—" She winced, trying to squeeze the word out.

"Pencils?" Zora said. There weren't any pencils here? This place was *called* Pencilvania. "I know I've drawn pencils before."

"Yes, and we used to have them in the store," Hazel said. "But once Viscardi arrived, we got rid of them all. Sharley gave them to Coco, who flew them over the Blank Bluff and dropped them. Anything dropped over the Blank Bluff is gone for good."

"Is Coco an airplane pilot?" Zora asked hopefully.

"Butterfly," Hazel said. Sharley was back with a Band-Aid, which he handed to the witch. "We also got rid of erasers, just to be safe, even though Viscardi prefers death by scribbling.

It's more dramatic." Hazel gently laid the bandage over Zora's cut. It was larger than a normal Band-Aid and cool against the heat of her wound.

"Thanks," Zora said. "It feels better already."

"You're welcome, dear," said the witch, patting Zora's hand. "With a mere drawing of a p-p-pencil, Viscardi could only draw scribbles to tie us up. What he's wanted all along is a *real* pe—a real pe—"

"A real pencil," Airrol said.

"Yes. And now he has one." Hazel leaned close to Zora. "I want you to know that we know that it was by accident that you brought a pe—a pe—" The witch rocked on her triangular base, gasping.

"A PEN—A PENNNNN—" the robot said, sparks shooting out of his neck.

"A drawing tool!" Airrol said, coming to the rescue.

"*Exactly*," said the witch. "Artists must carry drawing tools wherever they go. How were you to know it was dangerous to bring one here? If anything, you brought it to draw us something new."

"A TRAPEZE," Sharley suggested.

"A dance floor!" cried Hazel.

"Or a cake shop," Airrol said.

Zora scanned the sky for airplanes.

Hazel clapped her spider hands. "The dance floor could have a disco ball and strobe lights and—"

"I don't draw anymore," Zora interrupted.

"You mean you're not drawing at this *moment*," Hazel said. "How could you? Viscardi has your—"

"Pencil." Zora put her hand over the ridge in her pocket.

"*Yes.* But if you *did* have one—"

"It wouldn't matter if I had a pencil," Zora said. "I quit drawing."

"What?" Airrol said, sounding crestfallen.

"You quit?!" Hazel cried, throwing up her arms. Her stick-finger hands shot off her stick arms and rocketed into the sky.

"Oop," Airrol said, gazing up. "There they go." The two hands disappeared into the cluster of suns.

Hazel sighed. "It happens when I get overly excited or upset. They'll come back later."

"CHEER UP, SWEETIE," Sharley said, patting Hazel on the back with a claw hand. "LET'S DANCE."

141

"Good idea!" Airrol said. He turned to Zora. "Hazel is an amazing dancer."

"SO GOOD."

"Feel free to join in," said the witch. "You might get inspired to—you know—*unquit*."

Zora gave her a tight-lipped smile. Dancing was right up there with drawing on the list titled Things Zora Would Not

be Doing Right Now. She looked up at the sky. Where was that airplane?

"Hit it, Shar," said Hazel.

The robot used one of its claw hands to punch a sequence of buttons on its chest.

Boom,
pa-chhh.
Boom-boom
pa-chhh.

The beatbox grew louder, and Sharley's light bulb head flashed in time with the rhythm. The witch swung her stick arms in circles and rocked back and forth on her broad base, tipping up higher and higher on the two corners. Zora winced, waiting for her to topple over. Instead, she came to balance on one of the corners, then spun like a top.

Zora's eyes got wide. Hazel *was* a good dancer. Like, *really* good.

"Woo!" Airrol hooted, bobbing his neck to the beat. The motion rippled down to his four rear legs, his frontward and backward knees swaying side to side. He twirled his tail in a wide circle as his front legs did a fancy *step-touch, step-touch*. Zora stared openmouthed. Airrol was a good dancer. With those legs, who would've guessed? The rhythm started to infect Zora. Her fingers twitched. Her knees bobbed.

If Frankie were here, she'd bust out her signature dance move. She'd sink into a deep squat and start swinging her hips, flapping her arms, wrinkling her nose, and setting her teeth in a fierce dance face. Remembering this, Zora laughed and nodded to the beat.

If they were crabby or arguing, Mom would crank up the music for a Mandatory Dance Party. She said it was impossible to be in a bad mood when your body was moving to music.

The break-dancing witch struck a final pose, her handless arms crossed over her chest. Airrol's legs came to a stop. Zora clapped wildly. The witch took a bow. Her hands flew down from the sky and reattached themselves to her wrists.

Pop!

The music snapped off, and Zora caught herself clapping. What was she doing? Frankie wasn't here dancing. She was trapped in Viscardi's lair.

"Where's our airplane?" she asked Airrol.

Airrol cocked his head. "Good question. Oh, there's one!" He hurried across the street.

Zora's chest flooded with heat. *Finally.* She crossed the street behind Airrol, scanning the sky.

"Where is it?"

"Shhh. It's right here," Airrol whispered, inching toward a tree with a boxy brown trunk that grew out of the sidewalk. Landing on the solid-green pouf of leaves was an airplane the size of a dragonfly.

Questions crowded Zora's mind, each one fighting to be answered first. Why was the airplane so tiny? How would they get to Viscardi's lair before morning now? Why had they wasted so much time hanging out Downtown, chatting and dancing? One question cut to the front of the line:

"Why didn't you tell me airplanes are the size of bugs?" Zora demanded. "We can't ride in that."

Airrol widened his eyes. "I didn't know you wanted to *ride* in it. All airplanes are this size in Pencilvania." He gave Zora a sheepish look. "Are they supposed to be big?"

Zora sighed. "Yes."

A tiny door in the side of the plane hinged open. A minuscule dog drawn in colored pencil walked out onto the puff of leaves, dragging a hose. The pilot dog poked the nozzle deep into the green surface of the tree. Refueling, apparently.

Zora covered her face with her hands.

"I'm sorry," Airrol said. "I thought you had an idea to use an airplane to...I don't know. You're Zora. You've always got something up your sleeve."

"But I don't," Zora said and gazed toward the far-off mountain range. "How are we going to make it before morning now?" She imagined Viscardi scrawling an X over Frankie's small frightened face. Zora's breathing grew fast and shallow.

"No need to panic," Airrol said softly. "I'll carry you there."

Zora's eyes slipped across Airrol's backward knees and ankles, as if they were greased, and landed on the cross-hatched street.

"What?" Airrol said.

"Nothing. I just don't think that your legs could..."

Airrol bristled. "My legs?"

"They were a mistake, okay?" Zora blurted. "I was learning how to draw from life, and Mom told me not to peek at the paper, and the horse started moving and then you...you ended up with too many legs."

"Too many?" Airrol's spoony ears flattened against his head.

"I...I only meant to draw four. Sorry."

Airrol slowly rotated to the side. "Zora, look at my legs," he said. "*Really* look."

She fixed her gaze on his tangle of knees.

"I won the Horse Dash in the Pencilvania Games with a record time of eleventy-nine fourths," Airrol said, his nostrils flaring. "If I had fewer than seven legs, that wouldn't have been possible. Remember how I told you that Dee Dee, that blue horse your sister wanted to ride, was the second-fastest horse in Pencilvania? Guess who's the fastest?"

Zora raised her eyebrows. "You?"

"Yes." Airrol lifted his chin with the hint of a smile. "Thanks to you and your 'mistake.'"

"Can you get us to Viscardi's lair before dawn?"

"You can count on it."

Zora felt a tug in her chest to trust Airrol. "Thank you," she said.

Airrol bent his seven knees both forward and backward, lowering himself. "Hop on."

Zora took a deep breath, bracing for the memories that would engulf her when she touched him. She clutched a handful of Airrol's coarse gray mane and pulled herself onto his back. *Moving her pencil across the paper, her eyes glued to the horse by the fence. Mom right next to her, urging Zora to keep going.* Airrol smelled so strongly of newly sharpened pencils it made Zora's eyes water.

"Yoo-hoo!" Hazel waved from across the street. "Before you go, you must take something to eat." She teetered toward them, beige bread rolls speared on her stick fingers. Sharley clanked after her, balancing a two-tier cake on his claw hands. Zora's heart stumbled.

The cake Mom made for Frankie's last birthday. Zora had sketched it while Mom added the candles.

"CAKE FOR THE ROAD," he droned.

Zora's stomach yawned awake at the sight of the food. But no. She wasn't going to eat Frankie's cake, not when Frankie was probably so hungry herself.

"No thank you," Zora said quickly.

Airrol sank his teeth into the cake, coming away with a

goatee of white frosting. "Please eat something," he begged, his voice thick with cake. "We've got a long way to go."

Hazel reached for Zora, her stick fingers loaded with buns. Her hands looked like strange flowers.

"Thanks." Zora took a couple of rolls and stuffed them into her sweatshirt pocket. "For later." For Frankie.

Zora wound her hands deep into Airrol's grizzly mane and held on tight as the horse trotted down the street. His hoofbeat rhythm was different from the horses at North Shore Stables in Duluth. Airrol's seven hooves had a lopsided beat of *da-da-DUM, da-DUM-da-DUM* that tossed Zora back and forth so hard she had to squeeze her thighs tight against his flanks to keep from slipping off. But as Airrol increased his speed, the loud, chaotic rhythm smoothed to a quiet whir.

She peered over the side of Airrol. His legs were a soft gray blur beneath him, speeding his body forward.

"Whoa," Zora said. "You weren't kidding that you're fast. *You're* the one with special powers."

Airrol laughed. "I'm not the Girl with One Million Ideas."

"Do you actually believe in the Zoracle's prophecies?" Zora asked.

"I do."

"Why? You can see that I'm not two hundred feet tall, and my eyes don't shoot lasers. And I obviously don't have a million ideas." Not even close.

"I can't explain," Airrol said. "I believe because I believe."

Airrol glided swiftly across a wide, green field sprinkled with flowers, the blossoms nodding in the breeze. There were daisies and roses and sunflowers and tulips that looked like sporks. There were tiger lilies too. Mom loved tiger lilies. Zora heaved a heavy sigh.

Airrol tossed his head to the right. "We'll have to take the South Pass to Viscardi's lair, by way of the Baby Lakes. It's quite a hike, but don't worry—we'll get there before tomorrow morning."

"But what if Viscardi starts scribbling early?"

"He won't," Airrol said firmly. "He believes in the Destruction at Dawn with all of his scribbled heart."

"Why?"

"Because he's the star of it. So he'll follow the prophecy to a T and wait till dawn."

Zora bit her lip and nodded. At least there was that.

Zora adjusted her grip on Airrol's mane and turned to look back at Downtown, which was quickly receding. Were the skyscrapers...moving? A magenta one waddled like a penguin across the street. A blue one crossed in the other direction. The skyscrapers were slowly shuffling themselves like cards.

"Uh, Airrol? The buildings are moving."

"Of course they are," Airrol said. "They don't like to stay in one spot for too long. Who does?"

Buildings that walked. Airplanes that were tiny. Zora watched a cloud cartwheel behind a group of suns, which seemed to be playing Follow the Leader. "Why can't anything act normal here?" she said.

"Let me ask you something," Airrol said, gliding through a patch of multicolored roses. "When you draw something, do you pick what colors to use?"

"Yeah..." When she *used* to draw.

"Well, everyone likes to choose," Airrol said. "Everything you draw gets to decide what it's going to be and do in Pencilvania. When a drawing arrives, first they pick a name. To make it official, they tell the Zoracle. Then they get on with the business of being themselves."

"Wait, you named yourself?" Zora asked.

"Naturally," Airrol said. "It's my name. I have to answer to it. Shouldn't I pick it?"

"I guess." Zora had never thought about it that way before. She brushed her hand through a cluster of tall sunflowers, which nodded at her touch. "Why did you choose Airrol?"

"It just sounded good and felt like me," he said. "Why did you pick Zora?"

Zora's heart lurched. "I didn't. My mom named me."

Mom chose the name Zora because it meant "dawn."

Because you are my sunshine, she always said. The hopeful beginning of a new day. Now, the idea of sunrise made Zora's stomach go sour. *On the Blank Bluff at dawn, the pencil will end what must be ended…*

"I can't wait to meet your mom," Airrol said, wading through the dense blossoms. "A superhero, huh?"

"Yeah." Zora got a fresh grip on Airrol's mane as he powered up a hill. The wind ran its cool fingers through Zora's hair, and Zora closed her eyes. She imagined Super Mom tucking Frankie under one arm, Zora under the other. She flew them out of Viscardi's lair and sailed high over Pencilvania. In Super Mom's muscular grip, Zora felt safe for the first time in a long time.

But, Zora reminded herself, this superhero wasn't the only version of her mom in Pencilvania. As much as Zora wanted to find Super Mom, she didn't want to run into Sick Mom. She must hate Zora for drawing her at her worst. A terrible thought made Zora's ears ring. What if Sick Mom was on Viscardi's side?

"Ow!" A sharp pain on Zora's leg yanked her out of her daydream. "Something bit me."

"Gotta watch out for the scribbled flowers," Airrol said, wading through the dense blossoms.

Zora stared down at a fuchsia tulip, which was snapping its pointy petal teeth at her. Its stem and leaves were wound with dark-green scribbles. The tulip lunged, trying to bite her again. Zora lifted her leg out of reach and examined her ankle. It was bleeding.

Airrol sucked in a breath. "Those toothy ones are nasty. *Ouch!*"

A scribbled blue tulip had clamped down on one of Airrol's front legs. He flicked it off. Three gray trickles of blood ran down onto his hoof.

"This field gives me the creeps," Zora said. A rustling in the foliage caught her eye. A small black-and-white creature leaned its potato-shaped body back on the strong, flexible stem of a daffodil and...

Zing!

The stem launched the creature into the air. "Eeeeee!" it cried, sailing toward Zora like a dodgeball in gym class, its dot eyes and permanent smile speeding straight at her.

The Eeep hit her leg and clamped its chopstick arms onto

the seam of her jeans. She kicked, trying to shake it off. But the creature held on tight, using its stick arms to pinch the fabric of her pants.

"Get off me!" Zora cried. She gave her leg an extra-hard jerk, and finally the Eeep let go. Its potato-like body landed with a soft thud in the flower patch.

"Aw, it's just an Eeep," Airrol said. He gently prodded the creature with his hoof, helping it to its feet. "They're like babies, Zora. They mean no harm."

"It attacked me," Zora said. The potato person looked up at Zora, its dot eyes boring into her. What did it want?

"It was probably just trying to hug you," Airrol said. "Weren't you, little guy?"

"Eeeee," the creature said, opening its stick arms wide to Zora.

"No," Zora said and turned away.

The field of flowers ended, and a forest began. Airrol wove through a maze of trees that Zora had drawn at all different

ages. There were three-year-old Zora's lollipop trees: eight-year-old Zora's trees with forked branches and individual fluttering leaves, eleven-year-old Zora's trees with shaded bark and detailed foliage.

Airrol walked past brown and green and gray trees, trees colored burnt umber and burnt sienna and raw sienna. There were violet and red and turquoise trees too. Branches covered in snow wove a canopy with branches just bursting into spring bloom and leaves burning with the colors of fall. There were apple trees and orange trees and even a tree hung with sandwich triangles.

Once, Mom took them on a nature walk in the woods, and Frankie said she was starving (they forgot to bring snacks). Frankie yelled, "I wish sandwiches grew on trees!" Zora pulled out her sketchbook and drew a sandwich tree and then Frankie pretended to eat the picture.

Zora giggled at the memory.

Airrol chomped loudly. "Good sandwiches," he said, his mouth full. "Want one?"

Zora's stomach answered with a growl, but she quickly said, "No thanks. Hey, when you eat food here, is it gone for good?"

Airrol swallowed. "No, it comes back. Just like the balloons come back for the ceremony each morning. Everything returns, unless it gets thrown off the Blank Bluff or scribbled by a real pencil." He nodded at the branch he had just plucked bare. "Tomorrow there will be sandwiches here again."

Zora touched the bare branch. Only maybe sandwiches wouldn't be here tomorrow. Because tomorrow, if everything went according to her plan, Zora would untie Super Mom, and Super Mom would rescue Frankie, then help Zora and Frankie get back to Pittsburgh. Once they were gone, Viscardi would surely carry out *his* plan to scribble out all of Pencilvania. Zora twanged the empty branch with her finger. It hummed a low, melancholy note.

Airrol entered a darker section of the woods, where the canopy was so dense the sunlight couldn't break through.

Airrol stopped cold.

Up ahead, all of the trees were scribbled. The branches reached for the sky like fingers, dark-green scribbles wound

through them like a sinister game of cat's cradle. The branch fingers were moving. A nervous pit formed in Zora's stomach. It was the same feeling she got before going into the haunted house at the Minnesota State Fair. Only now, the monsters were real.

"The only way out is through," said Airrol, his voice shaking. He passed a bone-white tree wrapped in murky-green scribble rope, and something clawed Zora's shoulder, making her gasp. A branch, like a bony hand wearing bracelets made of rotten seaweed, sprang back to the top of the tree. A wild noise shot behind Zora, like the screech of a marker across paper. She whirled. A scribbled branch clawed the air inches from her face.

Zora flattened herself against Airrol's neck. "Run!"

15

Airrol broke into a run, dodging through the scribbled trees, which trailed their cold branch fingers down Zora's spine. Zora buried her hands in Airrol's coarse mane, wishing it were deep enough to hide all of her. She squeezed her eyes shut and clamped her legs tight against Airrol's flanks.

After a long minute, warm sunlight caressed her cheek. She opened her eyes. The trees in this part of the woods were sparser and paler, done in watercolors and oil pastels. The scribbled trees were behind them, still clawing the air.

"We made it," Zora said. "What a relief."

Airrol chuckled. "Did you just make a tree joke? Re-*leaf*?"

"Did I?" Zora said, giggling.

"That's tree-mendous!"

Zora groaned. "What *acorn*-y pun."

Airrol let loose a high horsey laugh. "Good one!"

When Zora was eight or nine, Mom had given her a joke book full of puns and riddles. She had memorized a whole bunch of them.

"Tree puns are kind of dumb," Zora said, "but they do *grow* on you."

"Stop!" Airrol cried. "You're too funny."

"*Oak*-ay," Zora said. "I can't think of any more anyway. I'm *stumped*."

Airrol's laughter echoed through the trees.

They reached a clearing where everything was pencil gray. A stream sketched in graphite gurgled past ashy grass and silvery bushes growing on the banks. Slate rocks on the ground served as perches for shadow-colored birds. Everything was camouflaged with everything else. Even Airrol blended in.

"One-Color Creek," Airrol announced.

The spicy, woody scent of freshly sharpened pencils hung thick in the air. The smell made Zora's chest ache.

Airrol broke into a smile. "This place used to be hopping with horses and Eeeps. So many dance parties on so many sunny afternoons!" His face drooped. "That was before Viscardi started taking prisoners. Now, barely anyone dares to come this close to the mountains."

Airrol stepped into the creek and lowered his head to the water for a long drink. "Have some," he said. "It's delicious and cold."

Zora eyed the stream, and her throat tightened with thirst. But she wasn't about to drink gray water. "No thanks," she said.

Airrol burped. "Please have a drink, Zora. What will your mother say if she sees you all faint from hunger and thirst?"

Zora's stomach flipped at the mention of her mom. "She won't say anything. She's dead."

"No," Airrol said. "I told you. Viscardi won't hurt anyone until dawn."

"I'm talking about my real mom, not a drawing." Zora's chin quivered. "She died."

Airrol's mouth dropped open, gray water dribbling over his bottom lip. He stood very still, ankle-deep in the rushing gray creek. "Oh, Zora," he said. "I'm so sorry." The stricken look on his face reminded Zora of Frankie's expression when she found out that Mom had died. Zora's heart twisted in on itself.

She stared down at her shoes and the surrounding gray grass, which now looked strangely hazy and tinged with pink. The haze thickened into a glowing pink fog that swallowed her feet entirely, then rose to her calves. Zora bent to trail her hand through the fog. Her fingers left swirling pink eddies behind. "What is this?" Zora asked.

"The Rosy Fog," Airrol said, disappearing behind a cloak of pink. "I've heard about it, but I've never seen it with my own eyes."

The fog rose to Zora's neck, then her nose. It tingled in her nostrils and filled her ears. She blinked, trying to see Airrol, but the pinkness pressed against her eyes blocking out everything.

"I never drew this," Zora said. But then she remembered.

Mom and Frankie and Zora were lying on the living room rug, their heads almost touching. *Imagine a cloud of pink light surrounding your body*, said the soft voice on the recording.

Frankie giggled. "Mine is like bubble gum."

"Mine's cotton candy," Mom whispered.

Zora's was flamingo-colored, but she didn't picture her cloud around her own body, like the recording told her to. She imagined a huge plume of pink light around Mom. *Visualize it washing your body and your spirit clean of all traces of illness*, the voice instructed. *You glow with perfect health and vitality.*

At school, Zora would wonder and worry how Mom was doing at home. Was she strong enough to sit and sketch by the bird feeder or too tired today? Were her leg bones aching more or less than yesterday? In these moments, Zora would color pink clouds in her notebook and imagine them surrounding Mom.

Mom said the visualization would work and so did the lady on the recording and the people at the store that smelled like incense, where mom bought the CD. Zora had wanted to believe too.

But she didn't.

Zora swatted away the pink fog, which stung her eyes. Or maybe it was the tears. She started sobbing.

"Zora." Airrol's voice drifted through the thick fog. "Are you thinking about your mom?"

"It's my fault that she died," Zora choked out. She threaded her hand into her jeans pocket, pulled out the pencil shard, and ran her thumb over the jagged end. Her hand began to shake, an earthquake that traveled up her arm into her chest crushing her lungs. She gasped for breath around the sobs.

"How could it be your fault?" Airrol said in a soft voice.

"It is," Zora said, her words slurred with crying, her heart racing from the pencil in her fist. "She was pretending she was getting better, and she wanted me to pretend with her. But I couldn't. I was mad that she wasn't being honest about what was happening to her. So I drew a picture of how she really looked, and I showed it to her. And later that night, she died." Icy guilt flooded Zora's chest.

"I'm sure you didn't mean to hurt her," Airrol said. "You wouldn't hurt anyone on purpose."

"How can you say that?" Zora was shaking so hard now her teeth chattered. "You *know* I made Viscardi and the Scribs." She had wanted to destroy every last drawing.

"Yes, but..." Airrol stopped himself. He began again, in a firm tone. "Zora. Your mom taught you to draw the truth. I was there, remember? She said, 'Draw what you see.' You saw she was dying, and you drew that."

"I wish I didn't!" Zora's sobs ripped through the fog.

"You did nothing wrong, Zora." Airrol's voice was stern now. "Your drawing didn't kill her. She was already dying— you said it yourself."

The pink fog was turning streaky with wisps of white.

"She lied," Zora said. "She kept insisting she'd get better, even on that last day. But she knew she was dying. I saw it in her eyes."

Airrol took a deep breath. "What if she didn't lie?" he said softly. "Can't someone both believe they are going to get better *and* know they're dying?"

Zora swiped her wrist across her dripping nose. "What do you mean?"

"When you were drawing me, I heard your mom say that something could be technically wrong but perfectly truthful."

Zora stared out into the thinning fog, listening.

"Technically, she was dying," Airrol said. "But her perfect truth was that she was going to get well. Why would she prepare everyone for her death if she was planning to live?"

Zora sniffled.

"And *your* perfect truth was that you saw her dying," Airrol said.

Zora bit the inside of her cheek. What if Airrol was right? What if Mom wasn't lying, but telling her own version of the truth?

As the pink fog thinned, Zora could just make out Airrol's kind face, like sunshine piercing a cloud.

His eyes drifted down to Zora's hand. His smile vanished. "What's that?"

Zora had completely forgotten that she was holding something. A tremor climbed her arm and rattled into her chest.

Zora took a shuddering breath. "It's a pencil."

16

Airrol leapt out of the creek. "You had another pencil this whole time? Why didn't you tell me?"

"Because the other half of the pencil caused so much trouble," Zora said. "I didn't want to make things worse than they already are." Zora crammed the pencil shard into her pocket. The tremors stopped.

"But a pencil in your hands isn't trouble. It's good," Airrol said. "You don't need Super Mom to fix everything— *you* can do it. All you have to do is draw."

Zora hardened her gaze. "I told you: I can't draw anymore."

"But why not?"

"I lost my Voom."

"What's Voom?" Airrol said.

"It's...a kind of feeling." Zora raked her fingers through her hair. "I can't draw without it. I lost it when my mom died."

Airrol looked doubtful. "Are you sure you can't draw without it?"

"I'll prove it." Zora kneeled by a coarse rock that bordered the bubbling gray creek and pulled the pencil out of her pocket. A fiery panic ignited in the hollow beneath her ribs. She scraped the pencil against the rough surface of the rock to sharpen the lead, rotating the shaft every few strokes as the point grew sharp. Her lungs shriveled until all she could take were little sips of air. She pivoted to the large, flat stone beside her and poised the sharpened pencil over it. Her vision narrowed.

The world tilted.

She was going to faint.

"Zora!" Airrol ran up behind her to break her fall onto the rocks. Zora threw the pencil to the ground and slumped against Airrol, panting, till the panic faded.

"See what I mean?" Zora said.

"I do." Airrol sounded sad. "Are you okay?"

"Yeah." Zora got to her feet. "Just don't ask me to draw again."

"I won't," Airrol said softly.

Zora shoved the pencil back into her pocket. Super Mom was going to save Frankie. End of story.

She looked at the horizon, where the suns had lined up in a long row. One at a time, they dropped out of sight, like coins into a giant slot. When the last setting sun fell, an afterglow splashed up. Fuchsia, fluorescent pink, and tangerine bled across the sky like watercolors.

"Oh!" Zora said, the wild beauty of it catching her by surprise. Her eyes sponged up the rich, sweet colors.

"Before we go, please have a drink," Airrol said, nodding at the creek. "We've been on the road for hours. You must be thirsty."

Zora lowered her fingertips into the cool, rushing water. She could almost feel it running down her dry throat. But it was *gray*. Would it taste like metal? Dirt? She gave her head a sharp shake.

"Zora." Airrol gave her a long look. "Trust me."

"Okay, okay," Zora said, kneeling beside the creek. She cupped her palms in the chilly gray water. She raised her hands to her lips and suddenly she was gulping, then dipping her hands again for more. It was cold and a tad sweet, and it quenched her thirst, but there was more to it than that. As the water flowed down her throat, a calm settled over her.

"Good, right?"

"It's not good." Zora wiped her mouth on her sleeve. "It's *great.*"

Airrol threw his head back and let out a loud horsey laugh. "I'm glad you think so."

Zora smiled and patted his flank. "Let's hit the road."

Once Zora was on his back, Airrol turned toward the violet-colored mountain range, which loomed large up ahead. He broke into a gallop. His hooves pounded the ground, then quieted to a smooth whir. The glow of sunset faded and twilight fell. Three full moons rose in the blue-black sky, each one surrounded by crescent moons like flower petals. Planets rolled and bounced gently across the sky, like tumbleweeds. Mars was drawn in rich-red oil crayon, Venus was blue, and there were a few rainbow-ringed Saturns in different sizes.

Zora gazed at the flat expanse leading to the foot of the mountains. It glowed with countless silvery pools.

Zora pointed. "What are those?"

"The Baby Lakes," Airrol said. "They're among the first things to come to Pencilvania. See how they're all wibbly-wobbly around the edges? Babies draw the best lakes."

"There are so many," Zora said.

"At least twelvety hundred," Airrol said.

Zora took a deep breath, and a familiar, peaceful coolness filled her lungs. Lake air.

Every August, Mom would strap the silver canoe to the top of the red Ford Fiesta she had named Yvonne and hop on Interstate 35W. They'd head north from Duluth to the Boundary Waters, where the United States and Canada meet. Zora knew they were getting close when the four-lane freeway turned into a two-lane road lined with pine trees and then the one-lane Gunflint Trail. She'd roll down the window and get a face full of cool, clean air, even during the hottest part of August.

Minnesota has more than ten thousand lakes, most of them scattered up north, and a lot have really random names. Spoon Lake. Pickle Lake. Gift Lake. Tin Can Mike Lake. Zora figured that there were so many lakes to name the obvious ideas got used up fast (Long Lake, Lone Lake), so the lake-namers had to use whatever popped into their heads. Party Lake. Glee Lake. Pea Lake. Some of the lakes were so tiny they didn't even have names on the map. The namers really ran out of gas when it came to those.

On the drive home from last year's trip to the Boundary Waters, just a few weeks after Mom told them she was sick, Zora asked, "What's the weirdest lake name you can think of?"

Mom glanced at the semitruck passing on the left. Her long, curly hair was wild from a week of no showers. "Big Rig Lake."

"Chocolate Cake Lake!" Frankie said. "Milkshake Lake."

Zora laughed. "For Pete's Sake Lake."

Frankie and Mom were cracking up too. They played the game till they ran out of words and were just naming the lakes with sound effects like *Wooooop* Lake and *Phbbbbbbbt* Lake. Finally, Mom took a huge swig of Diet Coke and let out a long, super-loud burp and then said, "Lake." Zora and Frankie clutched each other in the back seat, laughing so hard Zora thought her insides might fall out. Frankie had gasped, "No more! My stomach hurts. I'm dying!"

Zora stared out at the vast field of moonlit Baby Lakes. *Hang on, Frankie. I'm coming.*

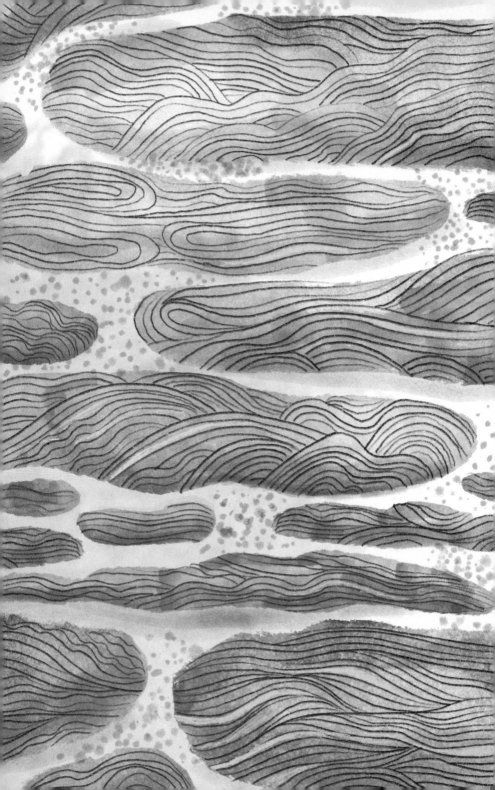

17

The countless Baby Lakes were packed close together, separated by thin strips of land that wove like a maze through the pools toward the foot of the mountains. Some of the lakes were a hundred feet or more across. Some were as large as the YMCA pool where Zora learned to swim. Some were as small as a bathtub.

With Zora on his back, Airrol stepped gingerly along a narrow walkway between pools. "I don't want to fall in," he said. "I can't swim, and I hear some of the Baby Lakes are very deep."

"Pittsburgh doesn't have any lakes," Zora said. "Zero. Unless you count Panther Hollow Lake, but I don't because it was made by people."

"The Baby Lakes were made by people too. You."

Zora laughed. "Good point."

"Oop!" Airrol's hoof slipped off the path and into a lake, nearly tipping them into the water. Zora clutched Airrol's mane as he scrambled back onto the slim strip of dry ground. He grinned sheepishly. "Close one."

"Hello there!" said a friendly voice.

Zora turned. A cream-colored pig rested its chin on its hooves at the edge of a small lake shaped like a banana. Water streamed off its pale ears and snout.

"Water pig," Airrol whispered to Zora. The memory of drawing the pig washed over her.

On the plane ride to Pittsburgh, the weekend before Mom went to stay at Allegheny Hospital. Frankie asked Mom a hundred questions (Do we really get a bunk bed at Grandma Wren's? Will she have good snacks?) while Zora stared out the pill-shaped window at the clouds, her sketchbook open on the meal tray. A cloud that resembled a pig floated by. She drew it.

"Whatcha up to?" the water pig asked cheerfully. "Goin' for a nice moonlight swim before the Big Scribble in the a.m.?"

"No," Airrol said sharply and picked up his pace. He followed the snakelike path between several lakes.

Splash!

The pig's head emerged from a large lake up ahead. Zora startled. Were the lakes connected underneath?

"Looks like you're headed for the mountains." The pig gave them a pitying smile and shook his head. "You'll never make it," he said in the bubbly tone that was getting on Zora's nerves.

"Thanks for the help," Zora said.

"I'm just stating the facts," the pig said. "See? The lakes are already moving. It's that time of night."

The pig pointed a dripping hoof at the lakes bordering the foot of the shadowy purple mountains. The silvery pools drifted toward each other and softly knocked edges, then floated away and knocked into other pools. It was like bumper cars in slow motion.

"Uh-oh," Airrol said.

Zora watched the paths between the distant pools narrow, disappear completely, then widen again. She slid off Airrol's back.

"It's no big deal," Zora said. "They're moving slow enough that you can tell when a path is gonna disappear. If one starts getting narrow, we'll just run a little faster. Come on."

Zora led the way, jogging along the dark strip of dry land between two lakes that shone with moonlight and starlight. Airrol trotted close behind.

The pig appeared at the rim of a pear-shaped lake. "This is just the warm-up," said the pig. "Soon, they'll be zipping around like pinballs!"

Zora gritted her teeth, racing along a narrowing path. She could really do without the heckling. But the pig was right: the lakes surrounding them were shifting and drifting slowly, but the ones by the base of the mountains were starting to move faster.

"We'll make it," she called over her shoulder to Airrol. "We just have to hurry."

Maneuvering the disappearing and reappearing paths felt like running the fifty-yard dash and playing hopscotch at the same time. Some of the lakes were so small Zora and Airrol could leap right over them. But the closer they got to the mountains, the bigger the lakes became. With a growing sense of dread, Zora stared at the pair of giant lakes ahead. The path between them was about a block long and three feet wide, and it was starting to thin.

"Get on my back. I'm faster than you," Airrol said.

"No time," Zora said. If they stopped for her to climb on, the lakes would close in. She ran as hard as she could, arching her chest forward and willing her body to go faster. Just a few more yards until they reached the large patch of land ahead.

The path under their feet became as thin as a diving board, then a balance beam, then a ruler, but she was already on the other side, safe, and—

Ker-splash!

Cold water drenched Zora's back. She spun around. Airrol frantically cycled his three front legs, churning the water. Zora dropped to her knees and gripped the edge of the lake.

"Swim to the edge!" she cried. "I'll pull you out."

Airrol's mane billowed up around his face as he struggled to keep afloat. She remembered then—he couldn't swim.

Zora grabbed one of his front ankles. "I've got you," she said, towing him to the edge. "Just stay calm."

He flashed her a nervous, hopeful smile.

"Look out behind ya!" The water pig rested its pudgy, pale forearms on the edge of another large lake that was drifting toward Zora. The patch of ground she was kneeling on began to shrink.

"Airrol, you have to climb out," she said, lifting his hoof from the water. She planted it flat on the edge of the lake. "You can do it."

Airrol nodded, biting his lip. He shifted weight onto the hoof, water streaming off his mane. "Oh!" he cried, slipping back into the water.

Zora shot a look behind her. The other lake was getting closer.

She faced Airrol, thrust her arm into the water and grabbed one of his pedaling legs. She locked eyes with him. "Try again."

This time, Airrol managed to get two hooves out before—

ker–splash!

His body plunged back into the water. His nose bobbed beneath the surface, his mane fanning out. Zora reached both hands under his chin and towed his head to the edge. She laid his chin on her thighs. Now what? Airrol couldn't climb out on his own. He was too heavy for Zora to drag out. And the patch of ground where she kneeled was steadily growing smaller.

She turned to the water pig. "Please help us!"

"There's only one way across the Baby Lakes," the pig said with inappropriate cheer, "and only one who can do it."

"Who?"

"Zora." The pig shrugged. "Too bad you're not her."

"I *am* her."

The pig's eyes bulged. "Oh! You are." His expression sank into a scowl. "Do you even *know* the prophecy?"

"Of course!" Airrol spluttered. "Zora, you're She Who Makes Lakes Laugh."

"Say what?"

"It's one of the prophecies the Zoracle brought us." Airrol's eyes sparkled. "'She shall make the lakes roll with laugher, and they shall roll out of her way.'"

"Right," Zora said. "Just one problem. The prophecies aren't true."

"Shh!" Airrol darted his eyes side to side. "Even if you don't believe them, the lakes might."

Water slopped against Zora's shoes, and she looked behind her. The other lake was almost here. In a minute, the narrow strip where she kneeled would be gone. She cupped Airrol's chin. What would happen to him if she fell in the water too?

"Zora," Airrol said, breathless from pedaling his legs. "Crack up the lakes like you cracked me up with those tree puns. I'm *rooting* for you." He gave her a quick smile, then went back to panting.

"This is no time for jokes," Zora said.

"This is *precisely* the time for jokes. Make the lakes laugh, Zora."

Zora's heart hammered in her chest. Could she both doubt that the prophecy was true *and* hope that it was? Why not— what did she have to lose?

She closed her eyes and pictured the joke book Mom had given her. She took a deep breath. "Knock knock."

"Who's there?" Airrol gasped.

"Water."

"Water who?" said Airrol and the pig.

"Water you doing in our way? Please move!"

"Ha!" Airrol wheezed. "That's hilarious!" The lakes didn't seem to think so. Not one giggle.

"They can't even hear me," Zora said. Lakes don't have ears.

Tiny ripples rose on the surfaces of the lakes, like goose bumps.

"They're listening," Airrol said. "Do another one."

Zora nodded. "What did one lake say to the other lake?"

"I don't know," Airrol said, panting. "What?"

"Nothing, it just waved!"

Airrol tried to muster a laugh, but he was too out of breath. The lakes were quiet too. Worse, the lake behind Zora was now just inches away.

"Tough crowd," said the water pig.

Tears pricked the corners of Zora's eyes. How many hours left till Viscardi scribbled out her little sister? Not many. And here she was, playing comedian to a bunch of lakes that weren't going to laugh because they were made of water, but she couldn't stop now because making them roll with laughter was her only hope for getting to Viscardi's lair, to Super Mom, to Frankie. Not to mention saving Airrol, who had been nothing but nice to her and was now panting so hard from cycling his legs in the water he seemed on the verge of passing out. The strip of land where she kneeled was so small now that the toes of her shoes were wet from the neighboring lake.

"Come on, laugh!" Zora demanded.

No reaction.

She stretched her lips into a ridiculous face, which always cracked up Frankie.

"It's not working," the water pig pointed out.

Frustration roiled in Zora's belly and shot out her throat as a wild, guttural yell.

"GAAAAAAAH!"

The lake behind Zora sloshed back and forth, slapping the opposite shores with a *ha ha ha* sound.

"Oh, you think that's funny, me yelling my guts out?" Zora demanded.

The lake answered with faster sloshing, which sounded like giggles.

"Then get a load of this." Zora threw her head back.

"UUUUUUUGHHH! NAAAAAH! RAAAAAAAAAWR!"

She summoned every moment of frustration and anger and disappointment and helplessness she could remember and poured it all into her screams. Every time she tried to draw and couldn't. Frankie's ugly-cake, bus-pass, no-good birthday party. Seeing Mom's strength fade in the final weeks and not being able to do anything about it. Every night in the bunk bed at Grandma Wren's wishing Mom would come give them a goodnight kiss and knowing it couldn't happen.

Zora let out long howls and staccato shouts.

The lakes sloshed and splashed. Near the foot of the mountains, the largest lake swelled in the center, the water bulging upward with a loud *HAAAA* sound. Then another lake swelled, followed by more and more lakes until the air filled with the *HA HA HA* of the rising lakes.

"You're doing it!" Airrol said, water churning his tail like boiling spaghetti noodles. "Keep it up."

"RAAAAAAAAH!"

Zora cried.

"GUUUUUUUUH!"

The edges of the lake behind Zora curled up and snapped to the center like a window shade rolling up. In its place was a large swath of dry land.

"Cool," Zora breathed.

The far edge of Airrol's lake lifted like the crest of a giant wave, towering high above them. Zora's heart rate soared. By the looks of it, the water was going to crash down on both of them. Airrol's head grew heavier in Zora's lap. The lake was tipping itself up, up on its edge. Zora scrambled to the side as the lake poured Airrol onto dry ground, spilling none of its water in the process.

Snap!

Twenty feet in the air, the lake pulled itself into a tight tube and fell to the ground with a soft *pof*.

"Ha!" It was Zora's turn to laugh. "It worked!"

"Told ya," said Airrol.

She put her hand on his soaking-wet side. "You okay?"

"Never better," Airrol said, smiling. He got to his feet, water streaming down his gray sides like curtains of rain.

Zora and Airrol watched the rest of the Baby Lakes—all twelvety hundred—roll themselves up with laughter until they were nothing more than a scattering of tubes rolling and quaking with giggles. Where the lakes had been was bare ground, clear all the way to the foot of the mountains.

Zora grinned. The prophecy was true. Apparently, she *was* a lake comedian.

She gazed at the mountain range, with its layers of violet and gray. Clouds hovered near the peak, shot through with lightning. If all the prophecies were true, what about the Destruction at Dawn, which predicted the end of Pencilvania? Or the one that said Zora would save everyone with her one million ideas? The world couldn't be both destroyed *and* saved.

A rolled-up lake the size of a wrapping-paper tube bowled toward Zora. She stopped it with her toe.

"Zora!" said a cheerful voice. The water pig stood beside them, dripping. "I knew you could make the lakes laugh. Never doubted for a moment."

Airrol made a grumpy noise in the back of his throat.

"The prophecy says that the lakes are gonna unroll when they're done laughing," the pig went on. "So unless you want another swim..."

The tubular lake under Zora's foot unfurled, splashing itself flat.

"Time to go," Zora said. She pulled herself onto Airrol's back in one fluid motion, like she'd been doing it all her life.

18

Airrol crossed the newly cleared flatlands and started up the mountain. If it was harder for him to run up an incline than across flat ground, Zora couldn't tell. His seven legs whirred at their usual pace. As the slope grew steeper, Zora leaned forward and held onto Airrol's neck to keep from sliding off of him.

Every step brought them closer to Super Mom and to Frankie.

In the Prussian-blue sky, stars appeared. Some were tiny white and yellow dots. Some were five-pointed outlines, the kind Zora used to scrawl on her spelling quizzes next to the right answers. Some had many points, like the bursts on cereal boxes that said IRON FORTIFIED and 50% MORE FREE. The countless stars twinkled and spun.

"Sing something," Airrol said.

"Why?"

"You'll see."

"Sugar Crumble Crisp tastes just right,"

Zora sang. The commercial jingle was the only song Zora could think of. The stars overhead swooped and circled like fireflies. "They're moving! Wait, now they stopped."

"Because you stopped singing."

"It stays crunchy in milk till the very last bite."

The stars clustered into a giant constellation of a face that sort of looked like Zora. She laughed. "That's awesome."

Airrol's legs made a steady hum as they raced up the hill. "On clear nights," he said, "I like to sing to the stars and make wishes. Want to know what I wish for?"

"What?"

"*Wings.* I'd fly over the whole of Pencilvania and see everything you drew all at once. I wouldn't need to go full Pegasus or anything," he added quickly. "Just a modest pair in gray pencil."

"I don't—"

"I know, I know," Airrol said. "You don't draw anymore. But maybe you could wish for your Voom to come back."

Zora tipped her face up toward the stars, which were still. Even if she could wish for the Voom to return, did she want it anymore?

"I wish..." Zora trailed off. Only a few hours ago, she had wished that there was never any Voom to begin with and that she had never drawn anything. Then there would've been no Viscardi to kidnap Frankie.

Zora listened to the syncopated rhythm of Airrol's hooves hitting the ground. She relaxed as the sound reverberated up into her. The rhythm had sounded so wrong the first time she rode him, but now it settled deep in Zora's chest like her own heartbeat. If she never drew anything, Airrol wouldn't be here. Would she wish him away?

She reached down Airrol's sides and burrowed her fingertips into his coarse hair. He felt like a big warm paintbrush. He had brought her all this way, risking his life for her and for Frankie. She remembered the terror she felt at the lakes that he might slip beneath the surface and not come back up.

No. She wouldn't wish Airrol away.

"I wish..." she said. "I wish for Frankie to have a horse ranch when she grows up. She wants at least a dozen horses. She's been planning it since she was five."

"And what do you dream of doing?"

Zora blinked. "I don't know." She used to think she would be an artist. She'd illustrate children's books or paint canvases that hung in art galleries. But when Mom died, Zora stopped imagining the future because doing that meant creating a picture in her mind that didn't include Mom.

Wind whispered by, as warm and soft as bathwater. It smelled like a set of scented markers when all the caps were off at once. Zora closed her eyes and inhaled deeply.

Zora looked over her shoulder down the mountain. Far below, the Baby Lakes had unrolled themselves onto the ground, seemingly in a different order than before. The water sparkled with the light of at least twenty moons and thousands of stars. In the distance, Zora could see the clustered hills of the Zoracle and the pointy rooftops of the Blue Block. The lights of the Downtown skyscrapers glowed faintly. And beyond all that, the big lake surrounding Pencilvania shone like a silvery-blue carpet that Zora couldn't see across, even from this great height.

Pencilvania was beautiful, and Viscardi wanted to scribble it all out. Every grain of sand and blade of grass. He'd scribble the lakes, the suns, the hamsters, the horses—*Airrol*—until the whole world was destroyed.

No. That couldn't happen.

Zora sat up straight, realizing something. "Super Mom isn't just going to save Frankie and me. She has to save *all* of Pencilvania." It wouldn't be enough to simply escape Viscardi. "Super Mom has to defeat Viscardi."

"Can she?" Airrol asked.

"Of course." She was a superhero. She was made for this kind of thing. Maybe she'd snatch the pencil from Viscardi and squeeze it to dust in her mighty fist. Then she'd grab Viscardi's scribble rope and fly circles around him, until he was completely immobilized. Super Mom would have super powers—extra strength and flying—but she probably had other powers Zora didn't plan on. Zora gasped, realizing something.

Mom had been really good at drawing, so the superheroic version of her would be an absolute genius at it. She'd draw something that would stop Viscardi for good. She had to because everyone and everything in Pencilvania had the right to be. Nobody should take that away. Not Viscardi, not Zora.

After Super Mom stopped Viscardi, she could draw a doorway out of Pencilvania so Frankie and Zora could go back to the real world.

Zora lay down on Airrol's back, resting her head on his wiry coat. Airrol began to sing in a deep voice.

On the darkest night
In the open air
The stars shine bright
For they see you there
Yes, the stars know your name
Oh, the stars know your name

The song raised goose bumps on Zora's arms. The stars swooped and spun overheard. As Airrol's last note faded, the stars slowed.

"Sleep now, Zora," Airrol said.

Zora yawned. "I have to stay awake for Frankie."

"Sleep so you'll be strong for Frankie tomorrow."

Zora's eyelids grew heavy. Her limbs felt weighted. She would just close her eyes for a minute...

Something pricked Zora's forehead like a mosquito bite. She brushed it away. Another prick on the back of her hand. She opened her eyes and sat up. How long had she been asleep? She glanced down the mountain. The Baby Lakes were far below now. Airrol wasn't walking straight up the mountain anymore—too steep. He plodded along a skinny path that snaked toward the top.

"Looks like we're in for some nasty weather," Airrol said grimly. "Ow. Ow. Needle rain."

Zora gazed at the dark cloud overhead. Short dark lines

of rain flew at her like a swarm of bee stings. She shielded her face with her hand. Her palm burned with pinpricks.

She flipped her sweatshirt hood over her head, pulling the strings tight. Needles of rain bounced off her cheeks. Oversize drops of purple rain began falling from the clouds like a water balloon attack.

Ploosh! Ploosh!

They exploded on Zora's thighs, soaking her jeans. They pelted her arms and head. A needle of rain pierced a fat raindrop in the air, drenching Airrol's nose.

"Ugh!" he cried, snorting.

Thunder boomed and lightning bolts zigzagged across the sky. The number of needles and raindrops doubled. The downpour flooded the ground, forming a stream that rushed over Airrol's hooves.

"Hold on tight!" Airrol shouted over the rain. Zora wound her fists and then her wrists in Airrol's sopping-wet mane. He slipped and lurched along the muddy path.

Ping! Ping!

Tiny white balls pummeled Zora's back and collected on the ground. Hail.

"Eeeee!" A cry pierced the sound of the storm. Zora peered out into the wet, inky darkness. A bolt of lightning lit up the night. A small creature with a body like a potato flailed on its back, waving its stick arms and legs wildly in the swirling water. It opened its tiny mouth to gasp for air, then went under.

Zora's own breath caught in her throat. Was that the same Eeep she had shooed away in the flower meadow?

It was drowning.

Zora slid down Airrol's wet flank and landed with a splash.

"Zora, get back on!" he said. "More bad weather is coming."

"There's something I have to do." The water swirled around Zora's ankles as she waded over to the Eeep, which had bobbed to the surface again. Rain pricked and burst on her back. Zora grabbed the Eeep from beneath, its body giving like a jellyfish under her touch.

"It's okay, little guy. I've got you," she said. She unzipped

her sweatshirt, tucked the Eeep inside, and zipped it up again. The Eeep nestled against her rib cage and heaved a sigh.

"Get on!" Airrol cried. "Tornado!"

Tornado?!

A large black funnel descended from the clouds like a finger pointing them out on the mountain.

Zora scrabbled onto Airrol's drenched back, cradling the

Eeep inside her sweatshirt with one hand. Airrol's legs fired like pistons, sprinting away from the tornado's accusing finger. Zora turned to watch it drop on the path behind them, where it spun like a top. Airrol joggled to the right as a smaller twister dropped to their left. Zora tightened her grasp on Airrol's mane. Another twister dropped on their right. The tornadoes whispered like ghosts as they twirled past. Zora shuddered.

"Yikes," Airrol said. "Snow."

Zora stared at the giant snowflake cartwheeling down the path toward them. Why was it so huge and thick? And who ever heard of a storm that included every kind of weather at once?

"Ready?" Airrol asked.

Zora winced. "For what?"

"This." Airrol leapt high into the air, his three front legs stretching out straight in front of him. He landed on top of the ridge of the snowflake, his hooves paddling like he was logrolling. White curlicues of wind urged the snowflakes to roll faster.

"Steady now," Airrol coached himself. "And...leap!"

Airrol split-jumped onto the next snowflake. The path was now crowded with snowflakes bowling down the mountain. Airrol leapt from one flake to the next.

Leap, paddlepaddle leap!
Paddlepaddlepaddle leap!

It felt like he was running up the down escalator.

"Go, Airrol!" Zora cheered. "You got this."

With one final leap, Airrol landed on the ground. They watched the snowflakes reel off into the darkness. Zora patted the Eeep in her sweatshirt to make sure it was still okay. "Eeeeeee," it said softly. Airrol was right. Eeeps *were* like babies.

"Rain, hail, tornadoes, snow—what next?" Zora said.

"That," Airrol said in a terrified whisper.

The clouds parted like curtains. An eerie lavender glow rose over the crest of the mountain. Not sunlight, not moonlight. Something else. It made Zora's skin crawl with invisible spiders.

Airrol slowly walked toward the glow. A massive arch of red, orange, yellow, green, blue, and purple came into view. Dozens of smaller identical arches flanked the center one.

Airrol's hide rippled with shivers. "There it is. Viscardi's Lair of Despair."

19

Zora laughed out loud.

"What's so funny?" Airrol asked, his sketchy lines trembling.

"Viscardi's lair is just a big pile of rainbows?" Zora hopped off Airrol's back, landing on a patch of olive-green grass. "Rainbows are officially the least scary thing ever. They're right up there with marshmallows and puppies. And Eeeps." She tucked her sweatshirt into her jeans, creating a secure pouch for the Eeep, which seemed to be sleeping.

"Rainbows are all the colors at once." Airrol's voice quavered. "Think of that power. It's no joke."

"Okay, but...*rainbows?*" A smile danced at the edge of her lips. The fear that had gripped her a minute ago felt far away now. This wouldn't be so hard after all.

Airrol pressed his shuddering side into Zora's arm. "What's the plan, again? Find Super Mom, then what?"

"She's probably tied up, like Viscardi's other prisoners," Zora said. "All we have to do is find her and untie her, and she'll take care of the rest."

"I'm starving!" someone growled.

"Hide!" Airrol hissed and jogged behind a large brown boulder. Zora hurried after him, then peeked around the edge of the rock.

A T. rex skeleton with scribbles laced through its rib cage strutted from the center rainbow arch. A scribbled-out narwhal with wiener-dog legs waddled after the T. rex, sweeping its long horn side to side on the ground with a scraping noise.

"It's almost scribble go time," said the T. rex.

"Not for a couple hours," said the narwhal. "Let's go find a snack."

The T. rex shrugged its tiny clawed hands. "Who's going to guard the front gate if we're gone?"

"Chill out, man. We'll be right back. I just want a sandwich or something." The narwhal trundled straight toward Zora and Airrol's rocky hiding place.

"Uh-oh," Zora said and darted her eyes left and right. There was nowhere to go without being seen.

Then Zora remembered. She reached into her sweat-shirt pocket and pulled out the two bread rolls Hazel had given her. She hurled them toward the shadowy slope on the other side of the T. rex skeleton.

"What the..." The narwhal stopped in its tracks.

"Flying buns!" cried the T. rex, clomping after the rolls tumbling down the mountainside.

"Save one for me!" The narwhal shuffled after the T. rex.

Zora nodded at the unguarded rainbow arch. "Now's our chance."

Side by side, Zora and Airrol walked under the enormous rainbow arch, the entrance to Viscardi's lair. Zora held her arm protectively over the Eeep sleeping inside her sweatshirt.

Their footsteps echoed in the large, chilly cavern. The rainbow-colored walls of the cave made an eerie buzzing sound, like neon lights. Zora's scalp prickled with static, and loose wisps of her hair floated out to the sides, electrified. Sharp stalactites hung from the low ceiling like a thousand fangs, glinting with all the colors. Nervous sweat prickled in Zora's armpits. Okay, maybe rainbows *could* be scary.

On the far side of the huge, empty cavern was a small rainbow arch leading to a shadowy tunnel. Zora waved Airrol toward it.

Inside the passageway, it was darker than the world's blackest permanent marker. Zora felt her way along the damp wall, Airrol bumping alongside her. Super Mom and Frankie had to be at the end of the tunnel. Zora began to jog down the gloomy, narrow twists and turns.

"*Zora will come bearing a pencil.*" A sinister voice echoed down the tunnel. "*On the Blank Bluff at dawn, the pencil will end what must be ended.*"

Light spilled from the bend in the tunnel up ahead, illuminating a spot on the rainbow-streaked wall. The shadow of a horse stepped into the spotlight. Its mouth opened in a smile, revealing two long fangs.

"Welcome, Zora," Viscardi said, sauntering around the bend. His giant scribbled form filled the tunnel like a clog of hair in a pipe. His cruel laughter hit the tunnel walls, breaking into a hundred hollow laughs that swarmed around Zora and Airrol. Her legs begged to run away, but she couldn't. Super Mom—her one hope for rescuing Frankie—was at the end of the tunnel.

Viscardi whipped his tail in a circle, sending a scribble rope into the air. It formed itself into a lasso that dropped over Airrol's head. Airrol gave a frantic whinny.

"No!" Zora cried, reaching for Airrol.

Viscardi jerked his tail to tighten the rope around Airrol's neck. He jerked it again, and Airrol crashed to the floor.

Zora's heart thundered. This wasn't how things were supposed to go. "Super Mom!" she yelled. "Help!"

"Dear, dear Zora." Viscardi's dank breath curled around her. "I knew you'd change your mind and come to help me. At daybreak, we will end this world together. Let's start with this seven-legged loser." One of Viscardi's scribble ropes twiddled the pencil tip inches from Airrol's nose.

"Don't!" Zora swatted the scribble rope away. "Let him go."

Viscardi flared his nostrils. "Let me guess. You're here to rescue your sister." He clucked his tongue. "What a waste of your talents. And now you'll die alongside her."

220

A dark-green scribble rope shot from Viscardi's back and coiled around Zora's shoulders. It wound down her arms, pinning them to her sides. The rope was cold and smelled musty.

"Like it or not, you're a part of the Destruction at Dawn prophecy. Fight it all you want. The story will still end the same way." Viscardi took a step back, then—

wham!

He rammed his forehead into Zora's chest.

She toppled, straining her hands behind her as she tried to catch herself. But the rope bindings made it impossible to move anything but her fingertips. The back of her head smacked the floor. Everything went black.

20

Zora slowly opened her eyes. She was propped against a wall in a sitting position, her legs stretched toward the center of a large circular room. She blinked at the shadowy shapes lining the curved, rainbow-colored walls. A single dim light bulb swung from the ceiling. She tried to raise a hand to touch the sore spot on the back of her head, but she couldn't. Scribble rope bound the full length of her torso.

This must be the prisoners' room. Now she was a prisoner too.

Zora's heart quickened. Frankie and Super Mom had to be

here. She scanned the lumpy figures against the rounded wall. A koala, a small black horse, a pile of tied-up hamsters and Eeeps, an orange robot...

"Frankie?" Zora called out.

"Zora."

Zora jumped at the whisper that was so close it almost seemed to be coming from inside her own head. She turned toward the figure slumped against the wall right beside her.

Frankie's face was gray, her tiny wrists tied together in her lap. Her legs were bound too—scribble rope covered her knees down to her small red tennis shoes. She shivered in her thin T-shirt.

"Frankie," Zora said, trying to reach for her sister. But the scribble rope trapped Zora's arms tight against her sides.

"I knew you'd come get me." Frankie's voice was as thin as tissue paper.

"Where's Super Mom?" Zora whispered.

Thuddd.

A panda with monkey paws dumped Airrol like a sack of

garbage in the middle of the room. Airrol's seven legs were gathered with scribble rope into a sad bouquet. Viscardi strolled out from the shadows and gave Airrol a firm kick in the back, making Airrol yelp.

"Leave him alone!" Zora yelled.

A smile swept across Viscardi's face as he sauntered over to Zora and Frankie. "Aw, a family reunion. Someone take a picture. Oh wait, don't. *I hate pictures.*" He lowered his head until his wild spiral eyes were level with Zora's. "Do you want to tell your sister how you came to rescue her and failed, or shall I?" Viscardi's nasty laugh bounced off the dark rainbow walls.

Zora sat up straighter. "You're wrong. I drew Super Mom, and she's going to stop you." She forced herself to hold Viscardi's terrible gaze.

"Who, her?" Viscardi tossed a hoof to one side. Zora's eyes traveled to a pair of blue rubber boots, up muscular legs wearing orange tights and thick scribble rope, and across powerful arms also bound in scribbles. Super Mom's eyelids were closed, and her breathing was slow with sleep.

"Mom!" Zora cried. "Super Mom!"

The figure stirred but didn't wake up.

"Super Mom?" Viscardi laughed. "More like Sleepy Mom."

He turned to address the rest of the room, walking in a slow circle. "In just a couple hours, when the suns rise for their morning soccer match, I will use my pencil to scribble you all dead. Ha HA!"

Viscardi galloped toward the tunnel. A scribbled deer with forks for antlers, standing guard at the tunnel entrance, stepped aside to let Viscardi pass. The sound of hooves echoed down the passageway.

"Zora?" Frankie's eyes welled up. "I don't want to die."

"Listen to me, Frankie. You're not going to die. It's your *birthday*." Zora turned toward the woman in the blue boots, who was stirring. "Look who it is."

Frankie gasped. "Mom?"

"I drew her at the pancake house, remember?" Zora said. "She's gonna kick Viscardi's butt and get us out of here."

The shine returned to Frankie's eyes. "Good."

Super Mom raised her bound wrists and rubbed sleep from her face. She blinked at Zora, then pulled her chin back. "Zora?"

Zora's ears drank in the music of Mom saying her name. She knew she longed to hear Mom's voice again but had no idea how much. A strange sound came from Zora's throat. Her chest jerked with sobs.

"Oh, Zora," Super Mom said. "Come here."

Zora scooted closer. Super Mom lifted her bound wrists up and over Zora, clasping her in a muscular hug. "It's okay," Super Mom cooed, rocking back and forth. Zora leaned her tearful face on Super Mom's brawny shoulder, making a wet spot on her shiny orange cape. She wanted to stay like this for hours, feeling the vibration of Mom's soothing voice. But there was no time.

Zora lifted her eyes to meet Super Mom's. "Viscardi is planning to kill everyone with the pencil I gave him."

Super Mom nodded. "I know. It's terrible."

"Yeah, but you're going to stop him."

"Me?" Super Mom sounded surprised. "How would I do that?"

"I'll untie you," Zora said, scanning Super Mom's ropes for a knot. It wouldn't be easy to untie it with only her fingertips, but she'd manage. Maybe Frankie could help. "Once you're free, you can go stop Viscardi."

Super Mom pulled away. "The ropes can't be untied, Zora.

Once you're trapped, you're trapped." She lowered her voice. "If the guard discovers you trying to escape, he ties you up twice as tight."

"So what if he discovers you? Punch him out and fly away," Zora said. "Go find Viscardi and take the pencil so he can't hurt Pencilvania. Draw a cage around him or something... Why are you looking at me like that? You're a superhero."

Super Mom let out an incredulous laugh. "Me? A superhero?"

"She's a drummer, dude," said a green goat with a braided beard. He slouched against the wall a few prisoners away.

The blood drained from Zora's head. *A drummer?* "But you're wearing a superhero cape and tights."

"This? It's my drumming costume," Super Mom said. "If I

had my drum kit here, I'd play you something to prove it. Hang on." She used her heels to tap out a rhythm on the cave floor.

"Listen," Zora hissed through clenched teeth. "I get it. Everyone gets to choose who and what they're going to be in Pencilvania. But I drew you to be a superhero, and that's what I need you to be right now. Mom, if you don't stop Viscardi, everyone in this room is going to die. He'll wipe out all of Pencilvania."

"Zora, I'm a big fan, and I hate to let you down." Super Mom's gaze slid away. "But you have the wrong idea about me. I'm not a superhero, and I'm not your mom. My name is Tish."

Zora's whole body went cold. Super Mom was their only shot at getting out of here, and she wasn't going to help? She wasn't going to fly after Viscardi and crush the pencil to dust in her mighty fist? She wasn't even going to free Frankie or Zora. Because she wasn't Mom. She was a drummer named Tish.

Zora took a shaky breath and curled toward Frankie. Frankie, who was not going to make it back to Pittsburgh, not going to take riding lessons, not going to grow up to have a stable with a dozen horses.

"Now what?" Frankie said.

Zora avoided Frankie's eyes.

"We *are* going to die, aren't we?" Frankie asked.

The last of Zora's hope leaked down her cheeks. She wouldn't lie. "I think so."

Frankie collapsed into Zora's side and sobbed. "I never even got to ride a horse."

"I'm so sorry, Frankie."

"Enough chitchat!" shouted the deer guard, storming toward them.

Zora shifted her body until Frankie fell softly into her lap. She couldn't save her little sister. She couldn't even stroke Frankie's hair to comfort her in their last hour together. "Frankie, forgive me," she said.

"QUIET!" The deer guard's head loomed over Zora, the tines of his fork antlers scraping the wall.

Zora stared at his scribble-covered legs until he stalked back to his post by the tunnel entry. Frankie whimpered in Zora's lap. Soon, Frankie's ribs rose and fell with the slow, heavy breaths of sleep. Minutes that felt like hours passed. The other prisoners, including Tish, dropped their heads to their chests and snored. Airrol lay on his side, facing away

from Zora. Was he in pain? Something squirmed against Zora's stomach, deep under the ropes. The Eeep! Was it okay under all those scribbles?

"Eeeeeee," it sighed contentedly. Poor thing. It had no idea of the danger they were in. And it was all her fault. She had created Viscardi and given him a pencil. She had set his destructive plan in motion, and now there was no way to stop it.

"Zora."

Zora turned toward the hoarse whisper coming from the wall. A gaunt face leaned out of the shadowy row of prisoners. A tube snaked out of her nose. She was completely bald. Bony knees tented a hospital gown, and her skeletal wrists were wrapped in scribbles.

Zora's mouth dropped open. "Mom," she whispered.

"Mom," the drawing echoed, nodding. "I saw her when you drew me."

"Oh, right," Zora said and stared at the floor. Just like Super Mom, this drawing looked like Mom, but it wasn't her. She probably had a strange name too.

"You drew me," she said, "and then your mom looked at you and smiled."

"I know," Zora said, her face getting hot. All the feelings of that day came rushing back. The anger. The frustration. The guilt.

Sick Mom blinked her heavy-lidded eyes. "After you left, she said something. I heard it."

"She did? What was it?"

"The same two words you just said to your sister: Forgive me."

Zora searched Sick Mom's eyes for more. Forgive her for what? For being so deter- mined to heal that she couldn't think of dying? For the leukemia winning even when she tried her best to beat it?

Zora thought about what

Airrol had said in the Rosy Fog. Technically, Mom was dying, but her perfect truth was that she was going to get better. She hadn't been lying. Just hoping with all her might.

Zora looked at the woman who was both her mom and not her. "I forgive you."

"I forgive you," Sick Mom echoed.

Zora choked out a sob and nodded. It wasn't Zora's fault that Mom had died either. Nobody wanted it to happen. It just did. Zora felt the complicated tangle of anger and frustration and guilt in her chest dissolve, leaving a great emptiness inside her. Like an infinitely large piece of fresh paper.

Sick Mom smiled. Zora smiled back.

Then something exploded into the emptiness in Zora's chest, fast and fiery like the Big Bang. It billowed up into her head and rolled down her arms and legs, filling every inch of her, throbbing hard against the scribble ropes. The blazing energy pulsed in all ten fingers like it was chanting:

Draw, draw, draw.

The Voom was back.

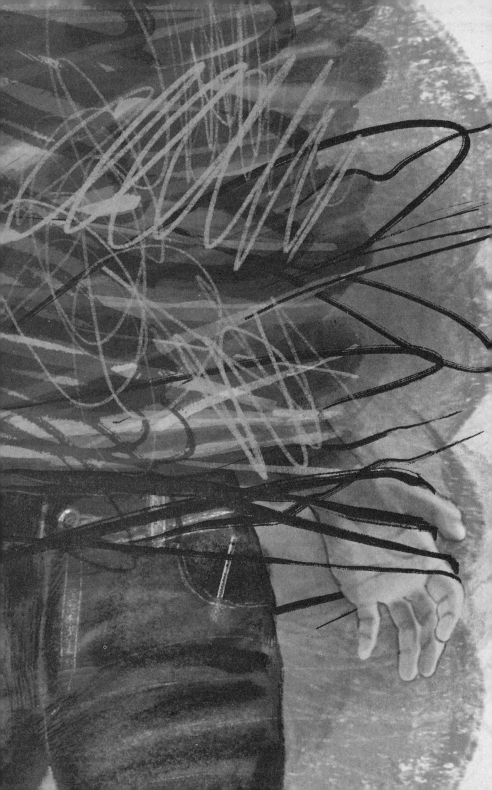

21

The energy surging through Zora's body was Voom times one
hundred. Voom times a *thousand*.

Zora's sudden urge to draw was like a mighty itch she was
desperate to scratch. She strained against the ropes binding
her arms, stretching her fingertips toward the hip pocket that
held the other half of the broken pencil. Could she reach it?

She hooked her thumb on the inside edge of the pocket
and pulled. The rest of her fingertips caught hold of the
denim, and she inchwormed her fingers into the pocket.
She rolled the smooth pencil shaft up over her hip bone.

When Zora finally grasped the pencil between her thumb and forefinger, she let out the breath she'd been holding. The Voom swelled.

The deer guard's hooves clip-clopped closer as he circled the prisoners' room. Zora glanced at Sick Mom, who mouthed, "Be asleep!" before shutting her eyes and faking a gentle snore. Zora did the same, forcing her breaths to come slow in spite of the Voom ricocheting in her chest like a million pinballs of light.

Zora slit one eye open. The guard stood at the tunnel entrance. He shot the prisoners a frosty glare, then turned down the passageway. His hoofbeats grew quieter, then louder, then quieter again. He was pacing in the tunnel.

A fresh burst of Voom coursed down Zora's right arm, an electric invitation that said, *Let's go!* Could she X out her scribble ropes? Too risky. There was no guarantee the X would only destroy the ropes and not her. She tapped her thumb on the pointy lead, which she had sharpened back at One-Color Creek.

Zora got an idea.

Tilting to the side, Zora eased Frankie off her lap and

onto the floor. Frankie snorted then sighed, still deep asleep.
Zora tipped herself onto her right side, so the fingers gripping the pencil rested against the cold stone floor. There was
no paper. Could she draw on the ground?

The thick ropes binding Zora's torso blocked her view of
her hand. She'd have to draw without looking. Her fingertips buzzing with Voom, Zora dragged the pencil tip across
the ground, picturing a shape in her mind. Straight line,
straight line, circle, circle. Her range of motion was small, so
the drawing would be tiny. Her fingers cramped around the
pencil tip. *Please work*, she begged.

There was a soft clink as the drawing became three
dimensional and real.

Zora laid down the pencil and picked up the small
pair of scissors. The finger holes were uneven and barely
big enough for her fingertips, but the blades lined up. She
strained her wrist to point the scissors in the right direction.
With a pinching motion, she worked the blades through the
first rope.

It frayed, then gave way with a puff of dark-green smoke.

Zora looked over at Sick Mom. She waggled her eyebrows

at Zora exactly how Mom used to when they were sharing a joke. Zora winked.

The deer guard's hoofbeats echoed softly, louder, then softly again. He was still pacing deep in the tunnel.

Zora made the miniature scissors chew through the next rope.

Poof!

A cloud of green scribble smoke that smelled of burnt rubber hovered around her face. She stifled a cough.

Her wrist had more freedom to move now. Cutting through the next rope was easier and faster.

Poof!

The scribbles binding her chest and shoulders slithered down her sides like snakes.

Poof!

They turned to smoke. Zora's ribs swelled with the first deep breath she'd taken in almost an hour. She grabbed the pencil and sprang to a crouch.

She was free.

Muffled hoofbeats in the tunnel grew louder. The deer was coming this way.

Zora looked over at Sick Mom, who was hazy behind the green smoke. Zora gave her a sharp nod, and Sick Mom returned it. The understanding that passed between them was as clear as if they had said it out loud.

Zora was going now.

Going to stop Viscardi.

22

Zora bent to give sleeping Frankie's cheek a quick kiss. "See you soon."

She scanned the rainbow-colored walls of the prisoner's room for tunnels or doors. But there was just the one tunnel, which the deer with fork antlers was guarding. There was no way she could sneak past him unnoticed—the tunnel was too narrow. His hoofbeats grew louder by the second. Any moment now, he'd march back into the room and see her standing here and then what? He'd tie her up again, alert Viscardi...

No.

She had to confront the guard in the tunnel.

Zora dashed into the shadowy passageway, the pencil in her right hand, the puny pair of scissors in her left. She stopped and frowned. What good were baby scissors against a giant angry deer with forks for antlers?

She could X him out with the pencil.

Swipe, swipe.

It would be easy.

But killing was Viscardi's thing, not hers. There had to be another way to get past him. Zora threw the scissors aside and crouched. In a Voom-fueled hurry, she drew a long, straight line, then a point, then another long, straight line on the gritty floor of the tunnel. When she connected the last line of the handle, the sword softly clanked into being.

Fork antlers cast a spiky shadow on the wall as the guard rounded the last corner. Zora snatched up the dark-green sword.

The furious deer towered over her. "What are you doing in here?" he barked. "Where are your scribbles?"

Trembling, Zora tightened her grip on the sword hilt. "Please let me pass."

"Not a chance," the deer said, tossing his head. The murky green scribbles tangled in his fork tines went airborne. A lasso took shape and flew toward Zora. She instinctively raised her sword. The lasso crashed into the blade.

Poof!

The scribble rope went up in green smoke.

"Oh, now you're *really* gonna get it." The deer spun another scribble onto one of his forks, like spaghetti.

Zora swiped at the deer's second lasso, accidentally slicing through the scribbles that bound his torso. The ropes hissed, then went up in a green cloud that reeked of rotten meat.

"My scribbles!" the deer cried. "You cut them all off!"

Time seemed to slow as the deer pulled himself up to his full height to tower over her, his huge body blocking the tunnel, fork antlers grating against the ceiling. As the deer stretched upward, the arch under his legs grew. If Zora ducked and ran under him, she could probably make it.

The deer dropped to a knee, blocking her escape.

"My scribbles are gone," he said, his voice filled with awe. Then he leapt to his feet and hopped lightly from side to side. "I'm free!"

Zora gaped at him. The scary, evil deer was...*dancing*? "I feel so light and loose," the deer said, doing a ballet leap. "Dance with me, Zora!"

Zora skipped in a half circle around him, bobbing her head, smiling, playing along, until the tunnel to the outside stretched behind her.

"Zora, you set me free," said the deer. "How can I ever repay you?"

"Simple." Zora said, her whole body pulsing with Voom. "Don't follow me." She turned and bolted down the tunnel.

"Done!" the deer shouted after her.

Zora sprinted down the dim passageway. She slashed scribble vines that hung from the ceiling, each one erupting in a satisfying puff of green smoke. What time was it? It had to be almost dawn. She ran faster.

What was her plan once she found Viscardi? How would she defeat him? Zora slashed another vine hanging in her way, and the answer became obvious. She'd cut off his scribbles. He'd start dancing and feel so happy to be free he'd want everyone else to be free too. He'd help Zora cut all the prisoners loose.

The tunnel widened into the main chamber of the cave, where she and Airrol had entered. Zora stopped short. Scribs were everywhere, sleeping in dark heaps. Her shoe brushed

the ear of the panda with monkey hands. It grunted. Zora's throat closed. But the panda's eyes stayed shut, and with a snort, it shifted back to sleep.

On the other side of the panda, the lion-dragon snuggled its scribbles like a blanket. Nearby the narwhal with wiener-dog legs snored so loudly its horn vibrated against the floor. Scribbled horses slept on their sides, packed tight across the floor like puzzle pieces. Dinosaur skeletons lay in a jumble of bones and scribbles, making it hard to tell where one creature ended and another began. The floor was carpeted with Scribs, all the way to the mouth of the cave.

How was she supposed to get by without waking them?

23

Zora surveyed the carpet of sleeping Scribs and rubbed the sword handle with her thumb. All she had to do was cut off their scribbles. They'd become harmless, just like the deer guard.

She raised her sword over the lion-dragon, then lowered it again. Wait. Even if she did manage to free a few Scribs, they'd make a racket in their giddy dancing glee. They'd wake the other Scribs, who would *not* be in a good mood, and they'd close in on her. No way could she cut off everyone's scribbles before that happened. They'd tie her up and drag her back to the prisoners' room.

Zora rolled the pencil between her thumb and forefinger. Voom rippled up her arm. Cutting off their scribbles wouldn't work, and she couldn't tiptoe through them—they were packed too close together.

Zora kneeled on the cave floor and chewed her lip. The pencil worked on solid ground, but what about in thin air? Her hand shook as she guided the pencil up six inches in the air, then over. The upside-down L she had drawn hung solidly above the ground. Zora exhaled.

A foot away, Zora drew another upside-down L, then connected the two with a horizontal line, forming a 3D step. She quickly sketched seven more steps as high as she could stretch on tiptoe and as close to the sleeping Scribs as she dared.

She circled back to the first step of the staircase. She tested it, leaning all her weight onto one foot to see if it would hold. It did. She silently jogged up the steps, the flat edge of the sword bouncing against her thigh. From the top of the staircase, she looked down at the mounds of sleeping Scribs.

You got this. Just keep going. Mom's words rang through her.

Zora touched the tip of the pencil to the edge of the last step. She had cleared the tallest Scrib by a good foot and a half. Now, she made a line parallel to the floor, like a tightrope, inching across it as she drew.

Zora was halfway to the mouth of the cave now. It was time to draw the steps going down to the ground. She began to draw the first step, then stopped.

A slide would be even faster.

But how could she draw a slide from up here? If she had two pencils, she could hold them out on either side, drawing the ramp a split second before she coasted down it. But she didn't have two pencils.

Directly below her, a scribbled black horse was stirring. Forget the slide. She needed an even quicker escape. The Voom swirled in Zora like a tornado made of fire. That's it—she'd draw a firefighter's pole.

Line, scoot. Line, scoot. Zora extended the tightrope as close to the mouth of the cave as she could. Then she drew a line straight toward the ground as far as her arm would reach. She grimaced. The only way to slide down was headfirst, her pencil outstretched, drawing the rest of the pole as she went. Was that even possible?

The scribbled black horse yawned loudly and lifted its

head. No time to worry if this was going to work. Zora slid the sword through her belt loop, securing it. She gripped the pole in her right hand—her strongest—and tipped herself upside down. Blood rushed to her head.

She plowed the pencil in her left hand toward the floor, making a line that wasn't quite straight but good enough. She loosened her grip on the pole and slid down a few inches. She tightened her grip and stopped sliding with a jerk. Now she was far enough along that she could twine her legs around the pole. Draw, slide, draw, slide. She was doing it. It was working.

"HEY!"

The sharp voice from below slashed Zora's concentration. She lost her grip on the firefighter's pole, and the room tumbled.

Crash!

She landed on something muscular and cold.

"A prisoner is escaping!" yelled the scribbled black horse. The scribbled pink horse Zora had landed on scrambled to its hooves, tossing Zora to the cave floor, her sword clanking.

Zora clutched the pencil and stared up at the two angry horses, who were quickly joined by more scowling Scribs.

"That's Zora!"

"Grab her!"

Zora leapt to her feet as the Scribs closed in.

She started to pull the sword from her belt loop, but the creatures crushed in so tight she couldn't lift her arm. Even if she could, there were too many Scribs here. No way she could slice through all their scribble ropes.

Bony claws grabbed Zora under her armpits and dragged her toward the tunnel leading to the prisoner's room.

"Stop!" Zora cried. "Stop, or I'll..."

"Or you'll what?" The monkey-panda leaned into Zora's face, sneering with rows of teeth that looked like corn.

Zora's mind raced.

"Or I'll...shoot you with my laser gaze!"

The panda flinched and pulled away. "No."

"Yes. I will." She glared at the T. rex skeletons that had her by the armpits. They released Zora, jerking their tiny arms to their chests. Their long pointy teeth chattered. "That's right. Stay back," Zora said. She turned in a circle, scowling. "Freeze right where you are and close your eyes! Or...or..." She wished she had listened more closely when Airrol was quoting the prophecy of the Girl with Laser Gaze. "Or you will get *lasered*."

The panda covered its face with its meaty monkey hands. The narwhal cowered at the feet of the lion-dragon, who trembled. All of the Scribs squeezed their eyes shut. Zora backed toward the mouth of the cave. She waved her hand in front of her eyes but didn't feel any laser beams. There weren't any. But the terrified Scribs, with their eyes closed, didn't know that.

"My laser gaze is on full blast now!" Zora boomed. "So don't you dare look at me. And don't move." When she reached the cave's opening, cool air teased her hair. But once she was out of sight, what was to stop them from chasing after her?

"To make sure you don't budge an inch while I'm gone..." Zora drew a giant circle in the air, almost as wide and as tall as the mouth of the cave. She darkened a smaller circle in the center of the large circle, then added scary veins for good measure. "I'm leaving one laser eyeball here."

The Scribs whimpered.

"And the eye's from the two-hundred-foot version of me,"

Zora said, "so the laser it shoots is no joke." She slapped the side of the eyeball.

Peeeeew!

A thick white laser beam shot out of the pupil and ricocheted off the far wall. The Scribs let out a group yelp. Zora raised her hand and caught the rebounding laser beam in her fist. It was warm but didn't hurt. She examined the cooling white line coiled in her palm. Her eyes *did* shoot lasers. Harmless lasers, apparently, but the Scribs didn't need to know that. She put the pencil in her pocket.

"I've got my eye on you!" she shouted, then dashed out of the cave.

24

Zora raced away from Viscardi's rainbow prison, down a wide path toward a broad nothingness that could only be the Blank Bluff. The sky was turning Frankie's favorite shade of pink. The suns would rise in just a few minutes. Zora pulled the morning air deep into her lungs. It smelled cool and clean, like new paper. Voom surged in her as she ran with one hand on the hilt of the sword, the other hand clasping her pencil.

She stopped.

Just ahead, the silhouette of a lone Scrib stood at the edge of the cliff, staring out into the endless blank. Behind one ear, secured in the snarled nest of his mane, was a pencil. It was sharpened to a deadly point.

Viscardi turned slowly to face Zora. He smiled, his dark fangs gleaming.

"Oh, my dearest darling Zora," Viscardi said in a tender voice. "Of *course* you escaped. Of course you came to help with the Destruction at Dawn."

"That's not why I'm here." Zora dragged the sword from her belt loop and walked toward Viscardi.

Viscardi smirked. "You found a sword, and you think you can stop me with it?"

Zora cocked an eyebrow. "*I'm* not going to stop you. You are."

She slashed her sword through the burly green scribbles around Viscardi's flanks. The ropes thudded to the ground, where they writhed and thrashed like pythons. Then—

poof!

His torso was wreathed in putrid green smoke. Viscardi tilted his head to one side, as if asking the smoke a question.

With a careful flick of the sword's tip, Zora cut the spirals from Viscardi's eyes. She trimmed away his fangs and sliced the tangles from his mane and tail. He let her. Viscardi's pencil dropped and rolled between his legs, stopping close to the edge of the cliff. The air was thick with green smoke and an incredibly sour stench, like garbage on a hot summer day.

Zora waved away the choking smoke. When the air cleared, Viscardi smiled a gentle, fangless smile. His perfectly traced eyes were clear and bright.

"Wow," he breathed. "You cut off my scribbles. Suddenly I feel so light and free."

Zora's shoulders dropped. "Good."

Viscardi looked at the sky, stained coral and copper by the approaching suns. "It's so weird. I don't want to destroy the world anymore," he said. "Instead, I feel like dancing around like a *dope*."

Viscardi's sudden icy tone covered Zora's arms in goose bumps.

"Yes," he went on. "I want to skip off with your ridiculous friends and stuff myself with pancakes and warble happy tunes." Viscardi pinned her with his gaze. Even though Zora had cut off the spirals, his eyes still seemed to spin.

Zora's pulse pounded in her ears. "I'm trying to help you," she said. "You don't have to be the way you are."

Viscardi tossed his silky purple mane. "But I want to be the way I am. Which is to say, I want to be like you."

"Like *me?*" Zora said. She and Viscardi were exact opposites.

"Who do you think showed me the power of scribbling things out?"

Zora flashed on an image of herself kneeling on her

bedroom floor at Grandma Wren's, green pencil in her fist, destroying one drawing after another.

Her cheeks burned. "But I've changed," she said. "So can you."

Viscardi laughed a brittle laugh. "Not gonna happen, sweetheart."

He used his flat front teeth to pick up his pencil from near the edge of the cliff. He drew a long, thick, green squiggle on the ground and nosed the rope up over his head. The scribble rope coiled around his shoulders and flanks, then wormed through his mane and tail. It settled into spirals over each eye and contorted into fangs, longer and sharper than ever. Viscardi shimmied his head and torso, settling the new, heavier scribbles into place. The end of the scribble rope plucked the pencil from Viscardi's teeth and held it aloft. His spiral eyes twirled in opposite directions, drilling into Zora.

"Ah, that's better," he said.

A shiver raced down Zora's spine. He *wanted* to be covered in scribbles?

Something wriggled against Zora's belly. The sleeping

Eeep tucked in her sweatshirt had been so still she forgot it was there. Now, it burrowed out from the waistband of her sweatshirt and dropped to the ground with a soft

plop!

Zora's breath skidded to a halt in her throat.

"Run away!" she said, thrusting both palms at the Eeep.

"Eeeeee." It smiled up at her, arms outstretched for a hug.

266

Flick-flick!

Viscardi drew an X on the Eeep's back as fast as a whip crack. The Eeep's potato-shaped body arched, its dot eyes fixed on Zora in surprise. It toppled forward. Zora dropped to her knees to catch it under its stick arms.

"*Eeeeeeeeeeeeeee,*" it cried like a balloon losing air. Its body slackened and began to shrink, smaller and smaller in Zora's helpless hands, until she was left holding only the green X. "No," she whispered. Hot tears sprang to her eyes.

"Oops." Viscardi coyly touched the pencil tip to his lips. "Was that your friend?"

Zora squeezed the cold, hard X. Viscardi was planning to do the same to the rest of the Eeeps. And Frankie and the Moms and Airrol and maybe even her too. Everyone and everything in Pencilvania.

No way would she let that happen.

Zora set her jaw and stood. The Voom pulsed in both arms, making the tips of her fingers tingle.

A long line of suns peeked over the edge of the cliff, flooding it with light.

"It's time, Zora dear." Viscardi squared his broad shoulders. "Thanks again for making me utterly unstoppable."

"You're not unstoppable," Zora said, steadying her shaky voice. "It's just that nobody's done it yet." She tossed the sword aside. It was useless against Viscardi.

Zora reached deep into her pocket and pulled out the other half of the pencil. She twirled it in her fingers like a miniature baton.

Viscardi's nostrils flared. "Another pencil?"

"Yep," Zora said casually, as if her heart wasn't galloping in circles in her chest. She held Viscardi's burrowing gaze and refused to blink. "Why, didn't your prophecy mention that?"

"So what if you have a pencil?" Viscardi snapped. "All you know how to do anymore is scribble. If anything, you'll use that pencil to help me."

Voom fired down Zora's arm. *That's what you think.*

"O Great Zora, please be careful!"

Zora whirled. Why was a hamster here? And it wasn't alone. A whole crowd of freed prisoners hurried toward the Blank Bluff, forming a half circle around Zora and Viscardi.

Scribs who had tried to stop her from leaving the cave were also there, their scribbles cut away.

"You left the scissors!" the deer guard called out to her. "I took the liberty. We came to help you. Hope that's okay."

"Thanks, Bruce," Viscardi said to the deer. "You brought an audience to watch Zora die. Even her baby sister gets to see the spectacle!"

Frankie was here? Zora frantically scanned the crowd. She met Frankie's wide, petrified eyes. Frankie held hands with Sick Mom, who held hands with Super Mom—Tish. Airrol and Dee Dee—the blue horse with a mustache—stood on the other side of Frankie, their scribble ropes gone. Airrol took a step toward Zora.

"No." Zora held up a hand. "Stay back, everyone. This is my fight."

"Ooh, great last words!" Viscardi said. His pencil danced at the end of his scribble rope. "This will be fun."

Zora rolled up the sleeves of her sweatshirt. "On my count."

At the edge of the Blank Bluff, ringed by a rapt audience of freed Scribs and freed prisoners—including Frankie and

Airrol and Sick Mom and Tish—with Voom lighting up every cell of her body, Zora said:

"One. Two. Three. DRAW."

25

Viscardi drew an X near the ground and punted it at Zora like a football. As it sped toward her, Zora sketched a box around the X. The shape began bobbing and darting in the morning breeze. A kite. Zora added a tail and grabbed hold. The kite lifted her high above Viscardi.

"Scribble as many Xs as you want, Viscardi," Zora said. "I'll turn them all into kites."

Viscardi glared up at her. "I *hate* drawing. But if I must draw in order to defeat you, then that's what I'll do." His scribble rope adjusted its grip on the pencil. "It's been amazing to meet my maker, Zora. Now prepare to meet yours."

Viscardi drew a lightning bolt, which shot through the kite, leaving a ragged hole. The force of the lightning strike pushed Zora out over the edge of the Blank Bluff. She plummeted into the abyss.

The crowd gasped.

As she fell into the blankness, Voom bloomed between Zora's ears. With a trembling hand, she drew a wiggly circle in the air beneath her. Her feet landed on the simple cloud, which hovered in midair, springy as a trampoline. She bounced once, twice, three times, until she had enough height to propel herself up over the edge of the cliff.

The crowd cheered as the cloud floated into view. Viscardi's ears flattened against his tangled mane. "So that's how it's going to be."

Zora jerked her chin up in a nod. "Get used to it." Hopefully she sounded way tougher than she felt.

Viscardi colored in her trampoline cloud with furious strokes, turning it to thick, choking smoke. Zora coughed and swatted the air. The crowd hacked and wheezed too. Without looking, Zora drew four large loops in the air, like a giant four-leaf clover. The fan blades rotated slowly at first, then went faster. They blew the toxic smoke off into the nothingness beyond the bluff.

Viscardi growled deep in his throat and drew a fireball. It rushed at Zora with a crackly whoosh. Her face began to toast. She reached out and drew waves and more waves—a whole wall of water. Viscardi's fireball hit the wall and sizzled to smoke.

"Gah!" Viscardi roared. He sketched a squiggly line that wound toward the water like a serpent. The line pierced the wall of water and grabbed Zora by the wrist.

Zora jerked her arm, cracking the scribble rope like a whip against the wall of water. The wall shattered. The force of the whip crack sent Zora reeling.

Bam!

She landed hard on her back.

"Give up," Viscardi commanded. "You know you want to."

Zora licked her bottom lip and tasted blood. Fighting Viscardi was hard. Giving up would be easy.

Directly overhead, the suns were gathered in a wide circle, unusually still. They weren't playing soccer. Were they watching the battle? Maybe even rooting for her? They all rushed to the center of the circle, then burst out like a firework. They *were* rooting for her. No way was she giving up now.

You got this, Zora told herself and got to her knees.

Viscardi drew a sharply pointed star and flung it at Zora. "Take that, loser!"

Zora ducked. The star sailed over her head and stuck—

twanggg

—into the large sun that had dropped low to catch it. The sun rotated and spat the star down into the abyss.

"I'm not a loser," Zora said. "In fact, I'm winning." She opened her arms to the crowd. "Aren't I?"

A cheer burst from the freed prisoners and freed Scribs. "Go, Girl with One Million Ideas!" came a deep shout that sounded like Airrol. Zora picked Frankie's high-pitched voice out of the crowd too. Zora's heart swelled.

Zora pointed at the sun that had stopped Viscardi's star. "Even my drawings are helping me. Everything and everyone here believes in me."

"Yes," Viscardi purred. "Everyone believes except me...and *you*."

"But I *do* believe," Zora said. "I'm the invincible one now. I can outdraw you all day long. You're done, Viscardi."

"Oh, really?" Viscardi leapt into the crowd and landed next to Frankie. He aimed his pencil at Frankie's small frightened face. His eyes spun at a dizzying speed.

"No!" Zora raced toward them, pushing her way through

the throng. There were too many creatures between her and her sister. She'd never get there in time. Any second Viscardi would X out Frankie.

Airrol stepped between Frankie and Viscardi, rearing up on his four hind legs. Viscardi tucked his chin and rammed the top of his head into Airrol's chest. Airrol cried out and collapsed. Viscardi grinned down at the gray horse, who was pulling in jagged breaths. The moms clutched each other, trembling.

"You BULLY!" Frankie cried. With both hands, she gave Viscardi's head a terrific shove. His pencil flew through the air, flipping end over end.

Zora shot up her left hand. She caught the pencil. Now she had them both.

"Give me my pencil!" Viscardi snarled.

"It was never yours."

Viscardi set his jaw. "You think I need a pencil to destroy your baby sister?" He nosed Frankie out into the open and toward the edge of the cliff.

Zora took a step toward them. "Don't."

"Stop where you are," Viscardi said. "One push and she's

gone." He prodded Frankie closer to the crumbly edge. To avoid going over, Frankie was forced to hug Viscardi's sinewy leg. "Give me both pencils, and I'll let her go."

Zora's mind scrambled for her next move. If she didn't give Viscardi what he wanted, he'd push Frankie off the Blank Bluff. But if she did give him the pencils, he'd keep scribbling things out. Frankie would die either way.

She squeezed the pencils in both hands. Where were the one million ideas now? The more she tried to think of what to draw, the more her panicking mind went blank, as empty as the white nothingness beyond the cliff.

That gave her an idea.

She lowered her eyes to hide their sparkle. "I give up," she said. "You can have the pencils."

"I knew you'd come to your senses," Viscardi said. He gave the crowd a fangy smile. "See? I win."

Zora raised an eyebrow. "The right time to brag is after you officially win. Don't you know that?"

Viscardi sashayed slowly away from Frankie and approached Zora. "Before, after, what's the difference?"

"Big difference," Zora said. "Huge."

Zora faced the cliff. She reeled both arms back, then hurled the two pencils far into the blankness.

"NO!" Viscardi leapt over the edge. His legs bicycled the empty air, and his jaws snapped trying to grab the pencils. He tumbled head over tail into the white void.

"MY PENCIIIIIIIIILLLLLLLLSSSSSSSSSSSSSss.

Viscardi grew smaller and smaller until he was only a dot, then not even that.

Zora stared down into the silent abyss.

"Is he gone?" Frankie asked in a small voice.

Zora pulled Frankie away from the edge of the cliff. "Yeah. He's gone."

26

Zora held Frankie by the shoulders, looking her over. "Did he hurt you?"

"I'm fine." Frankie beamed. "My sister's a hero."

"Zora is a hero!" someone yelled, and the crowd burst into applause and cheers. Eeeps gave each other high ones. Hamsters danced. Horses galloped in figure eights. Zora stood on tiptoe, craning her neck, searching for *her* horse. The image of Viscardi headbutting Airrol flashed through her.

"Airrol?" Zora called over the sea of bobbing heads and tails.

"Over there," the deer guard said, pointing with his fork antlers. Zora ran toward Airrol, and Frankie followed. A cluster of dinosaur skeletons parted, revealing an especially gray-looking Airrol lying on his side.

"You're hurt." Zora kneeled and rested a hand on Airrol's rib cage.

"He stunned me, but nothing's broken." Airrol carefully rolled off his side and onto his bent knees. "I think I can...easy now..."

He put one hoof on the ground, then another. Zora and Frankie pushed his belly from underneath, helping him straighten his four back legs and then the three in front.

"Thanks, you two," he said, shaking out his mane. He turned to Zora and stretched his lips to show every single one of his piano-key teeth, his smile as bright as a major chord. "You did it, Zora. You *drew*. You beat Viscardi!"

Zora laughed and threw her arms around his neck. She buried her face in his coat and inhaled the scent of fresh pencil shavings. It smelled like her mom and art and Airrol all at once. It smelled like love.

"I didn't do it alone," she said. "Thank you."

"Zora, the Girl with One Million Ideas," Airrol said, chuckling. "I told you the prophecies were real."

"Yeah...but..." Zora pulled back. "The Destruction at Dawn said the pencil would be used to destroy everything. 'On the Blank Bluff at dawn, the pencil will end what must be ended.'"

"Well, didn't it?" Airrol said.

Zora's mouth fell open. Yes. She had used the pencil to stop Viscardi, who had to be stopped. "So...Viscardi was wrong about what the prophecy meant," she said.

"I guess he only heard what he wanted to hear." Airrol smiled at Frankie as she stroked his mane.

"Did you know that the average horse heart weighs ten pounds?" Frankie told him.

"Airrol's heart is way bigger than average. More like twenty pounds," Zora said, which made Airrol laugh.

Two women approached slowly. The bony, bald one leaned on the muscular one for support. The hospital gown and cape fluttered in the morning breeze.

"Mom!" Frankie's voice cracked. She ran and flung herself into Sick Mom's skinny arms. Sick Mom folded Frankie into a

hug and stumbled back into Super Mom—Tish—who caught them both. "I missed you." Frankie sobbed into Sick Mom's shoulder as the two women rocked Frankie to and fro.

"Sweet baby," said Sick Mom, stroking Frankie's hair. "Everything's gonna be okay now."

Sick Mom's eyes met Zora's. She held out a bony hand and Zora took it. This was her mom. This wasn't her mom. She was gone, but she was here. She had done her best, which was far from perfect. As Zora held Sick Mom's hand, she felt joy and sadness and longing. But the feelings didn't swirl or roil. They rested quietly inside her.

Frankie pulled away from the embrace to look at Sick Mom, then Super Mom. "Why didn't you help Zora when she was fighting that mean horse? He was gonna scribble me out or push me off the cliff, and you didn't even try to stop him."

Sick Mom's chest caved. Tish stared at the ground.

"I needed *help*," Frankie insisted. "So did Zora."

"And you helped me," Zora said, putting her hand on Frankie's back. "So if I'm a hero, then you're one too."

Frankie's jaw went slack. "I am?" She marveled at her hands, the same ones that had shoved Viscardi's enormous head and sent his pencil flying. "Whoa. I am!"

Zora laughed. Sick Mom and Tish beamed grateful smiles at her.

"Attention, everyone!" a gray hamster cried from atop a fuchsia horse. The hubbub quieted. The hamster raised its paws. "It is time for the daily balloon release, then pancakes!"

"Pancakes?" Frankie squeaked.

She must be starving. Zora sure was. They hadn't eaten in what felt like weeks.

"Can we do pancakes first?" Zora shouted to the hamster.

"Absolutely, O Great One!"

Zora elbowed Frankie. "What are you waiting for? Go find your blue horse."

27

"I AM ON A HORSE!" Frankie cried, bouncing on Dee Dee's cobalt-blue back.

Zora laughed out loud. "Finally, right?"

Dee Dee grinned broadly under her curly mustache. "Hang on tight to my mane," she called over her shoulder to Frankie, then turned to Zora. "Don't worry, I'll be very careful with her."

"Thanks," Zora said and swung herself onto Airrol's back. Sick Mom and Super Mom—Tish—rode up close behind on a neon-green pony. Then Zora and Frankie, riding side by side on their horses, led the boisterous crowd of freed prisoners and freed Scribs down the sun-soaked side of the mountain. Airrol increased his speed, galloping at full power. "Woo-hoo!" he hooted, and Zora answered it with a joyful cry of her own. Dee Dee raced up beside them with Frankie, who was wearing the world's widest grin.

Tish started a chant:

Zo-RA! Zo-RA!

Frankie took up the chant and it spread through the crowd. Zora closed her eyes and drank it in. Even though Airrol was the only one carrying her, it felt like everyone was.

When they reached Downtown, hamsters and Eeeps and other creatures streamed out from the skyscrapers, joining the parade. Hazel and Sharley tipped and clanked from the Everything Emporium, the witch waving her arms so heartily her hands shot into the sky like fireworks.

Zora recognized the all-you-can-eat pancake house, with its familiar purple-striped awnings over the door and windows, on the shoreline right away. Inside, towers of steaming pancakes stood on every table, the aroma of vanilla and maple syrup and just a hint of crayon wafting from the food. The red vinyl booths looked as cozy as ever. Zora clasped her hands to her chest. In a world full of drawings that had the freedom to choose what they wanted to be, Zora was grateful the all-you-can-eat pancake restaurant chose to be just that.

"OMZ! I'm gonna eat a thousand pancakes," Frankie said, skidding into a corner booth. Zora and Tish and Sick Mom slid into the booth too. Airrol stood at the end of the table, already plowing into the stack of pancakes before him.

Soon, every booth and table was packed with Pencilvanians. Zora gazed around the restaurant, breathing in the memories along with the warm pancake smell. She savored them both. She saw:

A puffer fish with googly eyes. *The last time Mom took them to the Duluth aquarium.*

An elephant with heart eyes. *Valentine for Mom a couple years ago with the caption* Don't forget I love you.

A lime-green bird wearing big square glasses. Zora blinked, and a memory came rushing back. *Watching ore boats glide under the Duluth Lift Bridge in Canal Park. She and Grandma Wren waving at the sailors while Mom and Frankie threw popcorn to seagulls. Zora sitting on the back porch of their old house drawing this bird version of Grandma Wren, who cackled and said, "Zora, you captured me perfectly!"*

The green bird was happily forking pancake pieces into her beak. As she chewed, the fountain of lime-colored feathers on her head bounced. Seeming to feel Zora's stare, the bird turned to look at her. The bird raised a wing to her feathered forehead and gave Zora a salute. Zora returned the gesture.

Tish reached across the table and cut Frankie's pancakes into squares, just like Mom always had.

Frankie stuffed a bite into her mouth. "Mmmm," she said. "Zora, you have to try these."

With the side of her fork, Zora cut a fluffy wedge from her

own plate of pancakes. Her teeth sank into the perfect sponge, the syrup tingling on her tongue. Did pancakes always taste this amazing and she had never noticed before?

Ting-ting-ting.

The orange hamster in pink pajamas stood on one of the center tables tapping her fork against a glass. "I propose a toast," she announced. "To Zora, who not only created our world but also saved it!"

"To Zora!" chorused everyone in the restaurant, raising their forks in the air. The horses, unable to use forks, swung their tails. Zora spotted the snowman with carrot horns sitting at a table with the wolf wearing a basketball uniform and the half-finished drawing of a lemur. The protesters. Now, instead of shaking their fists at her, they lifted their forks in tribute.

Zora waved at them and the rest of the room. "Thank you," she said. "I also propose a toast. To Frankie. Yesterday was her birthday!"

"To Frankie!" shouted the restaurant, followed by more cheering and tail swinging and waving of forks.

Frankie couldn't contain herself. She stood on the seat of the booth and yelled, "I'm seven!"

The orange hamster waved its fork like a conductor.

"Happy birthday to you..."

As Zora and Super Mom and Sick Mom and Airrol and Dee Dee and the entire restaurant sang to Frankie, the world's widest smile spread across the seven-year-old's face. Before long, Frankie was doing her signature dance move: arms flapping, knees bent in a deep squat, hips wagging. The crowd clapped in time to the song and Frankie's dancing. Zora clapped louder than anyone. Now *this* was a birthday party.

When the song ended, Frankie collapsed against Zora in a fit of giggles. Tish and Sick Mom were laughing too. For Zora, it was a dream come true: her whole family laughing together again. Sort of. Close enough.

"Zora, you're like the queen of Pencilvania now," Frankie said. "That makes me the princess, right?"

Zora bit the inside of her cheek. *Queen?*

"If you don't want to call yourself the queen," Airrol said, "you could be the president or the prime minister or some other title you invent. It's your choice."

Zora nodded. It *was* her choice.

"You can be what you want, but I'm the princess," Frankie said. "And next year, when I turn eight, I'm gonna have my birthday party at the Ferris wheel—"

"Ah-ah." Tish wagged her finger. "You mean when you turn *seven*."

"No, I already turned seven."

Airrol licked his empty plate. "Then you'll turn seven again. Nobody gets older here."

"They don't?" Frankie said.

"Nope."

"Oh." Frankie set down her fork. Zora watched her sister think about being seven forever. No growing up to own a horse ranch. And Zora would always be twelve, never thirteen.

"What about getting taller?" Frankie asked.

"Nobody does that either," Airrol said. "Except Zora when she eats balloons. Then, her head brushes the clouds."

Frankie's face fell.

Sick Mom reached across the table for Frankie's hand.

"So what? That doesn't matter. You'll live with us on the Blue Block."

Zora thought about this. Everything in Pencilvania came from her. So if there was anywhere she truly belonged, that she could truly call home, it should be here, right? Grandma Wren's place in Pittsburgh sure didn't feel like home. Zora looked over at the goofy green bird wearing Grandma Wren's glasses. The problem wasn't that Grandma Wren was mean or terrible. It's that she wasn't Mom.

"You can each have your own bedroom," Tish said. "A whole floor, even."

"That's good," Frankie said, attempting a smile. "We have to share a bedroom at Grandma Wren's."

"Who's Grandma Wren?" Sick Mom asked.

Frankie blinked. "She's your mom."

Sick Mom shook her head at Tish, who said, "We don't have a mom. Nobody here does."

Frankie's eyebrows scrunched together. "What do you mean?"

"The closest thing we have to a mother is Zora," Tish said.

Frankie bit her lip and stared at the table. Zora gave a

heavy sigh. The drawings across from them looked like Mom. They sounded like her. They even seemed to love Zora and Frankie. But neither of them was really Mom. That person was gone.

Sick Mom tapped her bony breastbone. "You can call me Jules," she said.

Zora managed a small smile and nodded. "Jules."

"*Jewels*," Frankie said, brightening a little. "Zora, draw me a princess crown with lots of sparkly things in it."

Voom flared in Zora's chest, her fingers twitching, itching for a pencil. But wait. The two halves of the dark-green pencil had gone over the Blank Bluff. Sharley and Hazel had gotten rid of all the pencils Zora had ever drawn. And crayons and markers and paintbrushes—all dropped over the cliff. There weren't any art materials left in Pencilvania. She couldn't draw a princess crown or anything else.

The Voom throbbed in Zora's hands with nowhere to go.

She gazed around the restaurant at the hundreds of happily eating creatures. Zora had fought and defeated Viscardi so everyone—the Pencilvanians, Frankie, her—could live. For the residents of Pencilvania, being fully alive meant having the freedom to enjoy the world Zora had drawn and to choose what they wanted to be. For Zora, what made her feel truly alive was drawing. But without a pencil, Zora couldn't draw and couldn't be fully alive or truly herself in Pencilvania.

Neither could Frankie, who would stay forever short and seven here.

Frankie needed to grow up and run a horse ranch with twelve horses. Maybe twice that many—why not? Maybe Zora would live there with her. She'd sketch Frankie riding real-life horses. She'd draw trees and mountains and rivers. With every new drawing, Pencilvania would grow. She would grow. At the thought of this, Voom cascaded down both her arms.

Zora closed her eyes and felt the truth spread through her whole body. It felt right, and it hurt too.

We can't stay here. We have to go back.

28

The whole of Pencilvania paraded toward the grassy field for the balloon release ceremony. Joyful sounds bubbled all around Zora, but she rode Airrol in silence. Zora knew she and Frankie had to return to Pittsburgh, Pennsylvania. But how? She blinked up at the bright-blue sky. Scribble ropes had pulled her and Frankie in, and all the scribbles were gone now.

The singing hamsters led the massive parade onto the field. With all the freed Scribs, the crowd was twice as big as the day before. Eeeps and hamsters rode horses and dinosaur skeletons. The narwhal with wiener-dog legs and the deer guard, now free of their scribbles, marched beside Sharley, who carried a beaming Hazel in his vacuum-hose arms.

On one edge of the field, blue collaged waves rose and fell all the way to the horizon.

The singing hamsters scurried to the giant bouquet of multicolored balloons tethered to a boulder at the water's edge. The hamsters tugged the strings loose, then began handing out balloons to everyone. Airrol bent his seven knees, lowering Zora so she could accept a green balloon from a tiny brown hamster.

"Do you want an extra one?" he squeaked, offering an orange balloon. "You know, for a snack."

Zora started to say no, then stopped. How did the balloon-eating prophecy go? She eats them and then grows two hundred feet tall? Maybe if they could get up high enough, the sky would take them back? It was worth a shot.

"Thanks," Zora said and took the two balloons from the hamster. The rest of the hamsters, all holding balloons, formed a long line facing the crowd.

"At first, everything was blank!" shouted a tan-colored hamster in turquoise pj's. "At first, there was nothing, then there was a girl named Zora. Zora made a dot, then a line—"

"Wait." Zora slid off Airrol's back. "I want to tell the story this time."

"Of course, of course!" said the tan hamster. The hamsters scurried and scooched to make room for her in the line. Zora motioned for Frankie to join her. Frankie jumped off Dee Dee and carried her purple balloon over to the line.

Zora cleared her throat. "Once there was a girl. Two girls, actually. Sisters," she said, and Frankie nodded. "They were hungry. Hungry to do things, like take horse-riding lessons and draw. So they ate."

Zora brought the green balloon close to her mouth. Was this really going to work? She opened wide and pushed the balloon against her teeth.

Pop!

Lime-flavored air rushed down her throat. A strange feeling poured into her feet, like they were being inflated. She lifted the orange balloon to her mouth.

Pop!

She swallowed air that tasted like tangerines. Her legs lengthened a few inches.

"You're growing!" Frankie said, sounding jealous.

"The girls in the story ate," Zora called out to the crowd, then nodded for Frankie to eat her purple balloon. Frankie didn't hesitate. She sank her teeth into the balloon. *Please let it work for her too*, Zora thought.

"It tastes like grape soda," Frankie said, shooting up three inches. "More!" she cried, reaching for a yellow balloon.

"Yes," Zora said. "The girls ate more and more." She beckoned a group of hamsters over, accepting their balloons. She passed half of them to Frankie. Frankie chomped a red balloon and sprouted another three inches.

"The sisters grew and grew," Zora said, "until they were big enough to leave Pencilvania."

The crowd gasped.

"They *left*?" said the penguin in a top hat.

Frankie, who was now the same height as Zora, whirled on her. "Hey! We're not leaving."

"Certainly not!" said a white hamster. "Zora, you belong here."

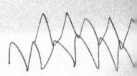

"More than any of us," agreed the stalk of broccoli. "Why would you ever want to leave?"

"So she can draw more pictures," called a familiar voice. Airrol stepped out of the crowd.

A knot swelled in Zora's throat. "That's right," she said. "Zora loved the world and wanted it to be alive and always growing."

A hush fell over the crowd. Some of the creatures stared at Zora, their mouths open. Some wept into their hands. Airrol gave her a sad smile but nodded his encouragement.

The tan hamster broke the silence. "Beautiful!" She clapped her paws wildly, her eyes teary. "The end!"

"No, not the end," Zora said. This was just the beginning.

"I'm *not* leaving!" Frankie shouted and bit into a pink balloon. She grew a head taller than Zora and glowered down at her. "We live here now."

"Frankie," Zora said softly, "do you really want to be seven forever?"

Frankie squeaked her thumb over the skin of a blue balloon. Her eyes filled. "No."

"Go give our Moms a hug." Zora's voice shook.

Frankie started crying. Sick Mom—Jules—shuffled over to her in her hospital slippers. Super Mom—Tish—strode toward Frankie too.

"Baby." Jules wrapped her thin arms around Frankie. "You're gonna be eight next year. Then nine, then ten. Double digits!"

"When you're all grown up, maybe you'll have a horse of your own," added Tish, stroking Frankie's hair.

"Twelve," Frankie sobbed. "I'm gonna have twelve horses."

"*Yeah* you are," Tish said.

Tears drew cold lines down Zora's cheeks. She knew Tish and Jules weren't really her mom. But still. Zora wrapped her arms around them and Frankie, joining the group hug.

"We'll always be here, cheering both of you on," Tish said.

Zora knew things could never be the same as before Mom died. But for the first time since then, she felt they'd be okay.

"Eeeeeee!"

Zora turned. A gaggle of Eeeps bounded toward her on their stick legs, their arms open wide.

"They saw the group hug," Airrol said. "They want in."

Eeeeee!

Zora kneeled, spreading her arms wide. The Eeeps crashed into her like a wave of squealing marshmallows. She laughed as they pressed their soft, squishy bodies against hers, clasping her with their tiny stick arms. It tickled, and it felt wonderful, like being covered with a hundred puppies. She gently folded her arms over the warm, squirming pile.

After a minute, the Eeeps tumbled off Zora and started giving each other gleeful high ones. Zora wiped her eyes, wet from both laugh-crying and cry-crying.

Airrol walked up beside Zora. His dark, liquid eyes looked extra shiny.

"I know you have to go," he said, his voice thick. "But I don't want to say goodbye."

Zora got to her feet. She rested her cheek on Airrol's bony nose and breathed in his smell of freshly sharpened pencils. "I don't want to say goodbye either."

"I'm so proud of you, Zora." Airrol's eyes were leaking gray tears. "And I love you. That's the perfect truth."

"I love you too." Zora gave his neck one last squeeze.

Then Zora led Frankie, who hung her head, back to the edge of the grassy field, the endless layers of blue water behind them. The hamsters stood nearby, holding more balloons out to Zora and Frankie. Zora accepted a pink one, brought it to her mouth, then sank her teeth into it.

Pop!

It tasted like a jelly donut. She grew a whole foot taller than Frankie.

Frankie scowled up at her. "No fair."

Zora handed her little sister a yellow balloon. "Let's see who can get to two hundred feet first."

The challenge sparkled in Frankie's eyes. She bit into the yellow balloon. "Lemonade!" she cried and shot up several inches.

Frankie gobbled balloon after balloon, as fast as the hamsters could hand them to her. So did Zora. The flavors of lime and strawberry and marshmallow and root beer mingled on Zora's tongue. Their bodies stretched tall and wide. Each balloon felt smaller than the last in Zora's mouth until it was like eating grapes. Soon, she and Frankie towered over the grassy field and the tiny creatures below. The horses swung their tails and hooted. Freed Scribs danced. The Eeeeps cried, "*Eeeeee!*" Jules waved, and Tish started up the chant again.

Zo-RA! Zo-RA!

From this great height, Zora could see all of Pencilvania. The mismatched, leaning skyscrapers of Downtown. The pointy roofs of the Blue Block houses. The heads of the Zoracle, which tilted up to watch her. Zora saw the twelvety hundred Baby Lakes at the foot of the hazy purple mountains, which were capped with a heap of rainbows.

She saw the beach where they had first landed in Pencilvania, the mighty Ferris wheel at its edge. As Zora and Frankie grew taller, the beach of multicolored dots below blended into a uniform beige, and the collaged layers of water surrounding Pencilvania became one brilliant blue. Zora was glad for all of it. Every last dot and line.

"Look," Frankie said, touching a cloud with a fingertip. They were near the ceiling of the sky. The suns scuttled around the girls' giant heads in what seemed to be a game of freeze tag. The light was brilliant. Zora kept her eyes open as long as she could then gave in and closed them. Her eyelids tingled with warm sunlight. The cheers from the crowd below faded, and a crackly noise grew, like a massive piece of paper being ripped in half.

FsshhhhhhhhhhHHHHHHHH!

Then silence.

29

Silence, then a saxophone solo. Jazz?

Zora opened her eyes. A ceiling fan slowly circled over-head. The fan blades weren't outlined in pencil or colored in with crayons. They were just...*real*. The bunk beds looked real too, the pillows and blankets full of detailed folds and rich shadows. She turned toward Frankie, who was stirring on the braided rug of their bedroom.

The balloon-eating worked. They were back.

Zora sat up. Outside the window, the sky was the color of the red row in a box of crayons—the scarlet and magenta and carnation-pink of sunset. The same sky as when they had been pulled into Pencilvania. How long had they been gone? Zora listened closely to the kitchen radio, with its wailing sax. Was that the same song that was playing when they left?

"Whoa, touch this," Frankie said in a spacey voice. She trailed her fingers over the braided rug. "This feels like an *actual rug*."

"It *is* an actual rug," Zora said. "Frankie, we're back."

"We are?" Frankie looked at the bunk beds, the fan, the closed door. Her shoulders sagged. "Oh."

Something crackled under Zora's hand. Paper. She scooted back, clear of the scattering of papers on the rug. "My drawings," she breathed. They were all here, just like she left them, except for one thing.

The scribble marks were gone.

Frankie's eyebrows tented as she scanned the pictures, searching for something. Not finding it, she sat back on her heels. "I miss her."

Zora scooted close to Frankie and wrapped her arms around her. "So do I."

"Can we ever go back?" Frankie asked.

"I don't know."

Frankie moped down at her outstretched legs. "I'm not two hundred feet tall anymore."

"Yeah. But you *were*."

Frankie grinned at Zora. "I was even taller than you."

"Knock knock," came a voice from the hall. "Can I come in?"

Frankie pulled herself into a tight ball. "No," she whispered, only loud enough for Zora to hear.

Zora turned toward the door. On the other side of it was Grandma Wren, who was practically a stranger. Who thought bus passes were a good replacement for riding lessons and who couldn't draw a horse with frosting to save her life. Also on the other side of the door: the closest thing they had to Mom anymore.

"Come in," Zora said.

The door creaked open. Grandma Wren stepped into the room as gently as someone can while wearing Frankenstein shoes.

"I heard shouting," she said, leaning against the doorframe. "I'd ask what's wrong, but you already told me."

Zora chewed the inside of her cheek. *Everything is wrong.* That's what she had yelled right after the worst birthday party in history. Right before they were yanked into Pencilvania with its talking horses and walking buildings and suns playing recess games. But all of the weird stuff in Pencilvania had grown on Zora. In fact, she already missed it. What if Grandma Wren and Pittsburgh could grow on her too?

"I don't know if *everything's* wrong," Zora said. "It's just... really different."

"We're still getting to know each other," Grandma Wren said. "It'll take some time."

Zora nodded.

Grandma Wren touched the top of Frankie's head. "But we'll get there. Won't we, birthday girl?"

"Grandma," Zora said, "Frankie needs horseback riding lessons. She's already a really good rider. I could do chores and earn money to help pay for the lessons and—"

Grandma Wren held up a hand to stop Zora. "Wait. You've ridden before, Frankie?"

Frankie gave several quick nods. "We both have."

"I didn't know that." Grandma Wren sat on the floor next

to them. "There's a lot I still don't know about you girls." She studied Frankie for a long moment. "Tell you what. There's a stable in Brighton Heights—it's just off my bus route. If they offer lessons for seven-year-olds, we'll sign you up. Deal?"

Frankie beamed. "Deal."

Zora slung her arm over Frankie's shoulders. "Thanks, Grandma."

Grandma Wren's smile slipped into a frown. "Zora! You're bleeding."

Zora looked down at her arm. Hazel's Band-Aid was gone. The slice from Viscardi's fang wasn't as deep as before, but a line of red still trickled from it.

Grandma Wren stood. "I'll get the first aid kit." She was back in a few moments with a gray metal box, which she opened at Zora's side. "Now let me see that cut."

As Grandma Wren cleaned the wound and dressed it with a large Band-Aid, Zora studied her grandmother's eyes behind her giant square glasses. Zora had never noticed before, but she had the same color eyes as Mom. Amber.

"There," Grandma Wren said, smoothing the edges of the Band-Aid.

"Thank you," Zora said, meaning it.

Grandma Wren reached for a piece of paper on the rug. She carefully examined the drawing of the deer with fork antlers. "This is good," Grandma Wren said. "Too bad you don't draw anymore."

"I do," Zora said quickly. "I mean, I started again."

Frankie slipped her hand into Zora's. Zora squeezed it.

"I'm glad," Grandma Wren said. "It's never too late to start over."

Zora smiled. "True."

30

Zora sat on her bunk bed, sharpening all of her colored pencils, except the dark-green one. That pencil was gone, the two halves thrown over the Blank Bluff in Pencilvania. She lifted the sharpener to her nose, inhaling the rich, bittersweet smell of wood shavings.

She opened her sketchbook—the old sketchbook of Mom's that Grandma Wren had given Zora on Frankie's birthday. Zora flipped past the sketches she'd made on Frankie's birthday bus tour around Pittsburgh: Croissants, which they stopped to buy at Market Square. The grassy bank of Panther Hollow Lake in Schenley Park. It was nowhere near as big as Lake Superior, but when Zora dipped her toes in it, the water felt cold and good. Lincoln School, where Zora and Frankie would start in the fall, just a couple weeks from now. Zora flipped to the palomino horse she sketched at Riverplace Stables—the last stop before they went out for pizza.

The stable *did* have riding lessons for seven-year-olds. And six- and five- and four-year-olds. That last part made Frankie mad, but she got over it as soon as Grandma Wren signed her—and Zora—up for weekly lessons. They'd go Thursdays after school.

Jazz music burbled from the kitchen radio. The notes still sounded like someone had thrown them in a blender, but oddly, jazz was starting to make sense to Zora. It was like the musicians were playing their instruments with their feelings more than their fingers. The sounds they made were strange but true. Wrong but right.

Frankie burst through the bedroom door. "Zora, check my line!"

"It's probably the same as yesterday," Zora said, hopping

down from the top bunk. Frankie asked Zora to measure her every day now, to make sure she was growing.

Frankie pressed herself against the doorframe and made a tall-looking face. Zora rested a light-blue pencil on top of her head and scratched a thin line on the wall.

Frankie stepped back to examine the line. "Whoa. It's totally higher."

Zora raised an eyebrow. The blue line was right on top of yesterday's pink line. If they measured every day like this, soon the lines would make a solid rainbow all the way up the wall. Which would actually look pretty cool.

Frankie ran out the bedroom door. "Grandma, I'm taller than yesterday!"

"See?" Grandma Wren's voice came from the kitchen. "It's all the vegetables you're eating. Want a carrot?"

"Yes!" Frankie dashed back into the bedroom with a carrot stick. She stopped in front of the cluster of framed drawings hanging in the corner of the room, where the moving boxes used to be. She stepped close to the sketches of the moms—Tish and Jules—which Zora had put together in one big frame. "Mom, look," Frankie said, then bit into

the carrot. She chewed with her mouth open. "See? I'm eating healthy."

With Grandma Wren's help, Zora had also hung the hamster slumber party scene—the only frame in the moving box that hadn't shattered when Zora dropped it. Beside it, in a small black frame, Zora's own face stared out at her, drawn in Mom's feathery pencil strokes.

When Zora had found Mom's portrait of her in the last moving box, along with the stacks of Mom's sketchbooks, she became a watery paint palette full of feelings: wistful purple muddled with yellow happiness and gray sadness.

But when Grandma Wren said, "I have an empty frame

that would fit that one perfectly," Zora said, "Good," and they hung it. Now, Zora smiled at herself on the wall. She shifted her gaze to Mom's framed sketch of Frankie reading *Horse Sense* on the couch, and a portrait Mom had drawn of herself a few years before she got sick.

If all of Zora's drawings went to live in Pencilvania, maybe Mom had her own kind of Pencilvania. Mom's world would be mostly silvery gray, full of wispy, realistic horses and trees and flowers and at least one huge body of water that looked like Lake Superior. Drawings of Frankie and Zora and Mom would be there too. And even if those weren't their names, at least they were together.

327

Did *everyone* have a Pencilvania?

Zora climbed onto the top bunk and sharpened the last pencil in the tin—turquoise. Voom buzzed in her right hand, ready. Good, because there was something important she had to do.

She reached for the piece of paper taped above her pillow. The picture of the gray horse with seven legs looked just like it had when she drew it months and months ago at North Shore Stables in Duluth. But it also looked different because she knew him now. Airrol was a friend.

Zora touched the tip of the turquoise pencil to Airrol's back, where she had spent so many hours riding through bright sunlight and pouring rain. She arced the line high, to the top edge of the paper, then curved it down. She drew the second wing to match the first. She added purple ovals and yellow spirals along the length of the wings, then she colored in everything else with orange. Zora taped the picture of Airrol with his new multicolored wings back over her bed. "Have fun with those," she said.

She opened her sketchbook to a clean page. Voom sizzled in her chest like a lit fuse, sparking a million ideas. A zillion possible drawings sped down her arm and buzzed in the tip of her pencil. Then an orange line raced out, cutting a bright path across the paper. Voom pulled her hand like a friend asking, *Wanna go somewhere together?*

Zora had no idea where they were headed or what kind of picture was coming. It didn't matter. Each new mark she made answered the question.

Yes.

Yes.

YES.

Acknowledgments

It took me over ten years to bring this book into being, and I had a lot of help.

I am indebted to everyone who read this story and gave me the feedback I needed to shape it, including Swati Avasthi, Heather Bouwman, Catherine Clark, Anika Fajardo, Jacque Fletcher, Ali Hensinger, Lynne Jonell, Rafael Kellman, Mary Logue, Mélina Mangal, Mitali Mangal, Katy Miketic, Kari Pearson, Paul Peterson, Annie Rollins, Jake Scott and his fifth graders (2013–2014) at Otsego Elementary, Trisha Speed Shaskan, Anne Ursu, Sarah Warren, Jacqueline West, and

Charlotte Sullivan Wild. My buddy-system buddy, Sarah Warren, deserves special thanks. She held my hand during the extended field trip of this novel and made sure I didn't get (too) lost.

Thanks to my wonderful agent, Carrie Hannigan, of HG Literary, for her support and enthusiasm all these years. Thanks also to Ellen Goff, Carrie's incredible assistant.

I am deeply grateful to Annie Berger at Sourcebooks, whose editorial insight helped me bring the story across the finish line. Thanks to Sofia Moore for her gorgeous illustrations.

A shout-out to everyone who provided childcare so I could go off and write, including Karen and Steve Watson, Lisa Watson, Dan Tanz, Angie Vo, and Keith Anderson.

Thanks to the Minnesota State Arts Board for the Artist Initiative grant that enabled me to focus on this book.

And thanks to my daughter, Ivy, for her love and inspiration. Ivy, you have more Voom than anyone I've ever met, and I'm so lucky to know you.

About the Author

Stephanie Watson is the author of several books for young readers, including *Best Friends in the Universe*, *Behold! A Baby*, and *Elvis & Olive*. In addition to writing, she loves teaching writing workshops and giving author talks at schools and libraries, both in person and online. She lives with her daughter in Minneapolis, Minnesota. Learn more at stephanie-watson.com.

About the Illustrator

Sofia Moore is a Ukrainian American artist and illustrator based in Las Vegas, Nevada. Inspiration comes to her from books, music, and world travels. She believes that children are natural artists and that nothing is impossible when pencil is put is to paper. Learn more at sofiamooreart.com.